The BLACK STALLION
and the LOST CITY

The BLACK STALLION
and the LOST CITY

Steven Farley

A Yearling Book

Text copyright © 2011 by Steven Farley
Cover art copyright © 2011 by Greg Call

All rights reserved. Published in the United States by Yearling, an imprint of Random House Children's Books, a division of Random House, Inc., New York. Originally published in hardcover in the United States by Random House Children's Books, New York, in 2011.

Yearling and the jumping horse design are registered trademarks of Random House, Inc.

Visit us on the Web! randomhouse.com/kids

Educators and librarians, for a variety of teaching tools, visit us at randomhouse.com/teachers

The Library of Congress has cataloged the hardcover edition of this work as follows:
Farley, Steven.
The Black Stallion and the lost city / Steven Farley. — 1st ed.
p. cm.
Summary: While in Greece making a film about Alexander the Great, Alec Ramsay and the Black Stallion get lost and find an immortal city ruled by the tyrannical, ancient Thracian god-king Diomedes, whose flesh-eating mare, not yet tamed by Hercules, takes a dangerous interest in the Black Stallion.
ISBN 978-0-375-86837-5 (trade) — ISBN 978-0-375-96837-2 (lib. bdg.) — ISBN 978-0-375-89887-7 (ebook)
1. Horses—Juvenile fiction. [1. Horses—Fiction. 2. Greece—Fiction. 3. Mythology, Greek—Fiction. 4. Motion pictures—Production and direction—Fiction.] I. Title.
PZ10.3.F215Bb 2011   [Fic]—dc22   2011001934

ISBN 978-0-375-87208-2 (pbk.)

Printed in the United States of America
10 9 8 7 6 5 4 3 2 1
First Yearling Edition 2012

To my family
and my animals

Contents

1

The Race Scene

Hollywood had come to the Balkans. Fresh off his latest sensational blockbuster, acclaimed director Stiv Bateman had set his sights on ancient Greece, Thrace and the story of the young king Alexander the Great. It was an extravagant picture with an extravagant budget, a cast of thousands and big-name stars. It also included the participation of Alec Ramsay—who many horse-racing fans considered to be a real-life young Alexander—and his horse, a real-life Bucephalus, a stallion known only as the Black.

Anyone who followed horse racing had heard about the mysterious Black, a horse as notorious for his personal history as for winning races. The Black's hatred of the whip was legendary in track lore. Rumors hinted the midnight-black stallion had even killed his previous owner, an Arabian tribal sheik, in revenge for mistreating him with a whip. And, as was fabled of the legendary Greek king Alexander and his black stallion

Bucephalus, it was said that no one but Alec Ramsay could ride the Black.

From his hilltop vantage point, Alec looked out over a wide valley crowded with horses, men and machines. They were high in the Rhodope Mountains of Bulgaria in a location that had been chosen just for this scene. It was in a seldom-visited part of Thrace, almost a day's drive from the production headquarters in the city of Xanthi, across the border in Greece. Before them, a thousand actors were taking their places on a prepared battlefield. The small army that was the film crew hung back along the sidelines among towers of lights and camera cranes.

Alec kept an eye on the Black, who nibbled at some grass as they waited together outside the wardrobe and makeup trailers. The stallion was carefully groomed and tacked up in a specially designed saddle, bridle and light armor. Flashes of sunlight danced off a polished copper breastplate lying against his coal-black chest. His ebony mane fringed the contours of his fine head and long, powerful neck, and his silky tail rose and fell behind him like the crest of a black wave.

Alec tried to hold the stallion steady as Leigh, a production assistant from the film's wardrobe department, crouched beside Alec's leg. She fiddled with the hem of his costume, a plain toga of fine linen.

"Keep still, please," she said through a mouthful of safety pins.

Alec did his best not to move, then closed his eyes as Harv, the makeup guy, dusted his face with powder. Through the lead line, he could feel the Black move his head beside him.

"Guess this has been pretty crazy for you," Harv said.

Alec popped open his eyes and blinked. "I'm not used to it," he said, "but it's been fun, really exciting. Who wouldn't want to be part of something like this?"

That was certainly true enough, Alec thought. How often do you get a chance to be in the movies? Even his parents and Henry Dailey had thought it was a great idea. "Take the money and run." Wasn't that what everyone had said he should do? It still amazed Alec that the film's publicity people had asked him to stand in as Alexander in a few scenes and had been willing to spend so much money to make it happen. Just for starters, his airfare over here with the Black must have cost thousands of dollars. Certainly it was the Black they really wanted, more than Alec himself. Few horses in the world could project his strength and beauty. It made Alec proud to think other people recognized this fact too.

Harv chuckled and gave Alec another swipe with the powder brush. Alec closed his eyes again and took a deep breath. No matter how well he and the Black were being treated, somehow he still couldn't help but ask himself what he was doing there—though it was a little late to be wondering about that now. He knew before he took this job that it wouldn't be as simple as everyone made it out to be.

Sure, he thought, everyone was nice, and the food and accommodations were first-rate, but all the waiting around was driving him crazy. As the producer had promised, Alec didn't really have to do much acting; he just had to show up for some riding scenes and a few stand-in shots like this one. So far, all Alec and the Black had done was some close-up work with the Black and an interview with Alec for a supplemental behind-the-scenes feature.

This time Alec and the Black were doubling for Alexander and Bucephalus in a shot that would lead up to one of the battle scenes. Bateman said he wanted a look that only the Black could give him.

A young woman carrying a clipboard walked toward them. "They want you on the set, Alec, whenever you're ready."

Harv handed Alec his bronze helmet and helped him get it centered and adjusted on his head and around his face.

Five minutes later, Alec and the Black were down on the set. Spread out before them were many, many actors and extras costumed as ancient Greek soldiers and armed with shields and spears. Some were assembled into blocks of infantry so tightly grouped together that they functioned as a single weapon, like a human tank bristling with spears. Behind the porcupine-like phalanxes of warriors stood hundreds of horses and riders, everyone waiting for the fanfare that was the signal to begin.

Marshals in golf carts shuttled between the different groups of infantry and riders, doing crowd control. Muscle-bound actors with long hair roping out from under their helmets argued and laughed. Sour-faced old guys watched the clock. Photographers' lights flashed as the actors and extras posed in the warrior outfits, everyone standing around, everyone passing time, waiting, waiting, waiting, everyone finding it almost impossible to stay busy. These were moments of patience for some, moments of nervousness for newcomers and a traffic jam of anticipation for everyone.

Alec's attention gravitated to the horses. He marveled at how many breeds were represented here. There were Arabians with flowing manes and tails, compact Andalusians and statuesque white Lipizzans. All were decked out in plumes, skirts of armor and breast and head plates, some with unicorn spikes, all meant to recall warhorses from ancient times.

Positioned along the edges of the battlefield, technicians were making last-minute adjustments. Some wore headphones and fiddled with soundboards. Others were hunched over consoles lined with blinking meters and dials. To one side, crane trucks with hydraulic lifts hoisted camera operators in baskets up into the air.

Alec took it all in, scanning the crowd for familiar faces. He recognized the producer Freddy Roth in his sport jacket and jeans, arms folded across his chest, eyes focused, apparently deep in thought. On the other side of the field, he saw Karst Balastritis standing with his sixteen-year-old son, Matt, and thirteen-year-old daughter, Xeena. The three were working for the production team, Karst as a top trainer and Matt and Xeena as wranglers and assistants. Matt and Xeena were doubling as extras and stunt riders too.

Karst was one of the first people Alec had met when he arrived in Xanthi almost a week ago. He was a proud native of this land, a big, gregarious man with dark hair and olive skin. Karst and his kids reminded Alec of a close-knit circus family—athletic, hardworking and full of energy.

Someone called his name, and Alec turned to see Jeff, the assistant to Freddy Roth. The skinny, young Australian wore aviator sunglasses and a New York Yankees baseball cap turned backwards. A jumble of laminated ID cards hung like medallions around his neck.

"There's been some rethinking about the schedule and the next scene," Jeff told Alec. "We just got the latest weather report, and they're calling for a chance of rain tomorrow. Stiv wants to stage the race in front of the assembled troops before the big battle scene now, when the weather is good, rather than risking a washout tomorrow. The course is all marked out down by the river. You know where I'm talking about?"

Alec nodded. "I walked it with Karst yesterday."

"Great," Jeff said as he started to hurry off. "See you there."

The last-minute change in plans was a pleasant surprise for Alec. He'd been looking forward to the race scene. Alec and the Black were to play the parts of Alexander and Bucephalus for the riding sequence and were to win the race. It would be a natural for the Black, Alec thought, and probably their biggest scene in the entire film. They wouldn't even have to act. If nothing else, it would be more exciting than the beauty-pageant posing he had been doing up to now.

A few minutes later, the horses picked for the race were grouped down by the river. Karst and the other trainers had done a good job in selecting the runners, and it was plain to see that these were some of the best-looking horses of the hundreds assembled there for the battle scene. Some were long-limbed and lean. Others were compact and solid. All looked fit, capable and ready to race.

Just off the riverbank in an idling speedboat, Stiv Bateman and a camera crew waited to film the race. The director, a burly man with a heavy beard, military boots and camouflage pants, sat in a raised chair near the bow of the boat. Two other camera boats were floating farther upstream. Radio static from walkie-talkies crackled in the air.

The horses lined up for the start at a spot marked by a strip of white tape on the ground. A short distance from where the tape ended, a heavy-duty pickup truck idled, ready to track the race from onshore. Mounted on the back of the truck was a small cherry picker. From his roost in a basket atop the crane's arm, a camera operator fiddled with his equipment, then leaned forward to frame up the shot in his viewfinder. Another team of photographers stood behind a camera on a tripod positioned in the grass. Next to them, the assistant director paced back and forth like a football coach on the sidelines of a big game. A guy holding a clapboard slate stood ready to identify the scene and take number.

Alec sat up and tested the spring in his stirrups. It didn't matter now that he was dressed in some silly costume of an ancient Greek king. This was a race, even if it was just a staged one, and Alec and the Black were in their element. Alec rested his face against the Black's neck, his eyes focused ahead, his knees pressed against the stallion's shoulders.

Once the horses were more or less in position, Bateman called out, "Okay, people. Get into character now, but wait for my signal to go. Ready. Speed!"

"Speed!" echoed the soundman from his position offscreen. The assistant with the clapboard stepped in front of the camera. "*Young Alexander,* scene seventeen-B, take—"

Suddenly there was a squeal from one of the horses. The assistant standing in front of the camera jumped back to get out of the way as two runners broke from their positions in line and charged ahead in a false start.

"I said to wait for my signal!" Bateman cried out impatiently.

Outriders caught up to the horses before they could get too far and helped steer them back to the starting line. Meanwhile, Alec and the other riders did their best steadying their mounts and keeping the line intact.

Finally the two runaways were back in place, and the sound and cameras started to roll once again.

"Action!" Bateman called from his perch on the bow.

There was an instant of relative stability and then they were off. The camera-laden speedboats in the river wound up their engines and moved out in pursuit.

Voices filled the air as the riders urged on their horses. A colt on the outside bounced out and half reared before his rider could set him on his way. The rest bolted off in a mad panic. In a split second, Alec had the Black after them.

The Black gathered himself and settled into stride. Alec coaxed the stallion along and guided him closer to the river's edge on his right. The Black felt good and was anxious to run after so much standing around over the past few days. The horses swerved and started to bunch up as they approached a bend in the river.

Alec did his best to hold the Black back. Bateman's instructions were for a come-from-behind win to the race, with a close finish. But, as always, once he got going, the stallion wanted to run all out. This was just another race to the Black, and he would do whatever he could to get out in front. Alec could feel the pull in the reins all the way to his shoulders.

As the horses swung into the right-hand turn, Alec switched modes and went from restraining the Black to encouraging him. The Black responded and they galloped into the middle of the pack, slowly gaining ground on the others.

Alec moved with the stallion as they came out of the turn. Edging farther to the inside, he pulled the Black just to the left of a big gray colt running hard a length off the water's edge. The Black paced the horse a moment, then started to pull away. Alec saw a lead runner directly in front of the Black was losing steam and coming back fast. He guided the Black to the right and started to drop in, just in front of the gray, moving to the inside slot along the river where there was a clear path to the lead.

Suddenly the gray's rider shouted a warning. There was someone running up the inside that Alec couldn't see! Even worse, with the gray blocking the view, the oncoming rider hadn't seen Alec make his move for the inside path either.

On a professional racetrack it might have been different. There the gray's rider would have known that it was his responsibility to give a heads-up to the other riders in such a situation, especially when two horses running hard on either side of him were making for the same spot and couldn't see each other. But this wasn't a racetrack and these riders weren't jockeys. By the time Alec heard the gray's rider call out, it was too late. The Black was already on a collision course with the inside runner, a big bay who was sprinting ahead like a mad demon and trying to squeeze his way between the gray and the riverbank.

Once he realized what was happening, Alec had no choice but to check the Black with a hard pull on the reins. It kept him from dropping in on the bay, but it was too late for the bay and the gray running next to him. Blocked to the left by the fading leader, and in front by the Black, the gray was trapped. He spooked and broke hard to the right, careening off course and taking the approaching bay with him. Instantly the two horses went flying over the riverbank, hitting the water six feet below with a mighty splash.

Over the clamor of grunting horses and shouting riders, Alec could hear Bateman calling out orders from one of the camera-laden speedboats that had been tracking the runners from the river.

"Keep the camera on them!" Bateman squawked over his bullhorn from his position on the bow.

Alec pulled the Black up and circled around to see if he could help the riders who had gone into the river. Down in the water the horses were shrilling. A minute later, they and their riders scrambled up a low spot in the embankment. Alec recognized one of them as Karst's daughter Xeena and suddenly realized she was the rider who had been caught on the inside when the gray spooked and charged the river. Thankfully no one seemed to have been injured in the spill beyond a few scratches and getting wet. Xeena and the gray's rider were already laughing it off. What a relief, Alec thought. He knew there was no way he could have prevented the accident, though he and the Black certainly had been a factor in causing it. In the end, there was no one to blame.

"That was terrific," Alec could hear Bateman call out to the riders from the water as they turned their horses back to the staging area. "Bonuses all around for you people. Now let's go back and do it again. Just try to stay out of the drink this time."

2

Acracia

The Rhodope Lodge, where Alec was staying, housed
a cavernous dining room, and that night it was packed
with cast and crew. Everyone was eating at different
tables, more or less self-segregated according to job
description—actors with actors, carpenters with carpenters, camera people with camera people. Alec took
a plate of food from the buffet and found a place with
some of the horse folk, Karst Balastritis, Xeena and
Matt. It was easy to see that the three were related. All
had the same curly black hair, broad shoulders, sharp
eyes and high cheekbones. And there was something
else, too, Alec thought, something in their bearing that
set them apart from the rest of the people here.

The Balastritises were speaking in Greek, but
when Alec joined them, they switched to English, a
language they all spoke quite well, especially Xeena
and Matt. Alec appreciated the courtesy, as he knew
only a few words of Greek. Karst watched him with

warm, friendly eyes and a smile that made people feel good every time he turned it on.

Matt was talking excitedly about how he had landed the job of wrangler for a scene Bateman was shooting the next day. It would mean an extra bonus for him. Karst was saying it was a lot of money for someone his age and that he shouldn't let the bonus go to his head. Karst's voice was stern, but Alec could see pride in the trainer's face as well.

"Go to his head?" Xeena teased. "Not Matt. He already thinks this film is really about him."

Her brother gave her a smile and laughed. "Please, little sister," he said. "I am just doing my job here. You should do yours and try to keep from riding your horses into the river."

Xeena's eyes flashed. "You know that wasn't my fault," she said. "You saw it, Alec. Could I have helped what happened during the race? What choice did I have? It was either go into the river or get run over."

Alec nodded his head in agreement. "It looked that way to me."

"Let's just say I'm not surprised that if somebody had to go off course, it would be you," Matt teased.

Karst held up his hands. "Enough, you two," he said in his thick Greek accent. "Everyone doing fine and no one blaming anyone for anything. Now quit fighting and eat your dinner."

Halfway through the meal, Jeff, the producer Roth's assistant, came over to their table. Jeff congratulated Alec on his ride that day. He said the scene looked great, and the footage of the accident was a real bonus. Bateman was saying that the horses flying off the riverbank and splashing into the river had turned out to look spectacular.

"And tomorrow?" Karst asked Jeff. "I hear there is big schedule change."

Jeff laughed. "Yes, well, big changes at the last minute seem to be par for the course with Stiv."

"Hokay," Karst said. "You the boss."

Jeff smiled and shook his head. "I'm just a link in the chain on this job, like you. Anyhow, the word is that now the weatherman says it's not going to rain tomorrow after all. That means the crew will be splitting up into three different units—red, blue and black. Matt, you are staying here to work on the battle scene with the red and blue units, like we talked about earlier."

Matt nodded eagerly.

"Alec, you and the Black are with the black unit and will be heading up into the mountains. The trip will probably take most of the day, depending on the road conditions. Once you reach the location site, you'll spend the night there. The following day, after the scene is set up, Stiv will helicopter in and supervise the shot."

Jeff asked Karst and Matt to go over to Bateman's table and meet with some of the camera and lighting guys. They wanted to talk over some particulars about the different shots they were planning for tomorrow.

"So, what is the place we're going to?" Alec asked Jeff after Karst and Matt left to meet with Bateman.

Jeff sat down at the table with Alec and Xeena. He took a roll from the bread basket. "Some monastic refuge in a place called Acracia," he said between bites. "It's supposed to be beautiful there. Lots of wildlife, some small forest reserve up in the mountains, no roads, no houses or towns the cameras would have to work around. Just unobstructed views, trees and wide mountain vistas, much like what the area might have looked like back in Alexander's day."

"Sounds great," Alec said. "Where is it?"

"Up on Mt. Atnos," Jeff said. "It's in an area that is usually closed to the public. It took months to get the okay to film there, and we had to pay a hefty fee. The permission just came through, which is another reason for the last-minute change in plans. The monks don't allow cars on the premises, so we have to stay at a compound outside the monastery. There is no electricity either. We'll manage with our generators, though."

A moment later, Karst and Matt came back to their table.

"Alec and the Black are going up to Mt. Atnos tomorrow," Xeena said excitedly, "to the monastery in Acracia."

"Boss say I go with them," Karst said. "You come too." From the way the family exchanged glances, it was obvious the names meant more to them than just spots on the map.

"I still can't believe it," Matt said. "I didn't think the monks let anyone up there anymore."

"Me neither," Xeena said.

Karst shook his head. "I no believe it too. Boss must have pay much, much money."

"I wish I was going with you," Matt said, "especially after all the stories Popi used to tell about those woods when we were little."

"You have'a your hands full right here," Karst said. "You do good job, make family proud." His eyes shifted to the exit. "Now we go for sleeping. We wake up early tomorrow."

Shortly after daybreak, crews worked to get the convoy of horse vans, camera cars and equipment trucks in the black unit ready to set off for Mt. Atnos. There were about a dozen vehicles in all, including a truck carrying a cargo of snakes that were to play a part in a scene planned for the black-unit shoot. As the cages were being loaded onto the truck, Conrad, one of the snake wranglers, showed Alec his favorite one, a four-foot-long leopard snake he called Litzy. Conrad draped her around his neck and cooed gently to the snake as if she were a beloved pet. Like her breed's namesake, Litzy had spotted markings, and Conrad maintained that her species was the most beautiful of all European snakes.

"Looks like a viper but she ain't," Conrad said in his heavy British accent. "You can tell because she don't have the vertical pupils. See? Most all vipers have vertical pupils." He held the snake's head up so Alec could see the shining black stones of her eyes. "Want to hold her?" Conrad asked.

Snakes didn't bother Alec as they did some people, but he wasn't interested in having one crawl around his neck just then. "No thanks," Alec said. "The Black is sensitive about snakes. If the smell gets on me, it might startle him. I love her leopard spots, though. Very stylish."

Conrad chuckled. "She's a beauty, all right," he said, then gently returned Litzy to her cage.

Alec turned and started to where the Black was stabled. Jeff was sitting in a golf cart parked beside the line of trucks and vans and waved Alec over. He looked at Alec and smiled. "Don't tell me—Conrad was showing off his pets again?"

Alec laughed and asked Jeff about the snakes and

what they had to do with the story of Alexander. Jeff explained that the snakes were part of the film's dream sequence they would be shooting the next day.

"In the dream, Alexander's mother has a vision of her yet-to-be-born son as a two-year-old," Jeff said. "The child is alone, lost in the mountain wilderness and threatened by snakes." Jeff shook his head. "Stiv loves snakes," he explained, "and always tries to work them into his films if he can."

Alec soon saw that, aside from the snakes, there were a number of other animals the black-unit crew was bringing to the mountain shoot with them. There were a few stable ponies for riding horses, a pair of big bay geldings and a beautiful dark-brown, almost black Andalusian mare named Tina that was standing in for Bucephalus in some scenes, like the Black. In addition, there were a couple of goats for background scenery, four or five ducks and a pair of trained weasels.

Finally all was ready and the convoy started off. Alec and the Black rode in Karst's van. Xeena sat on the bench seat between Alec and her dad. Every so often, Alec checked on the Black by peering over the partition into the stallion's stall in the back of the van.

Soon they came to the switchback road that led

up the mountain. Karst expertly navigated the van over the narrow, winding road while Alec looked out the window at the unspoiled forest below. With Xeena's help, Karst passed the time by explaining to Alec that this area was renowned as the homeland of the mythological singer Orpheus. Even now it was fabled that there were enchanted woods here in which whole cities could hide and never be found. There were other tall tales about places that had no deer, squirrels or birds, places shunned by humans and forest animals alike, places where a stream of poisoned water would madden or kill any animal that drank from it.

Karst laughed. "All crazy talk, stories for children. No reason be afraid. Water good here. Best in Thrace. Plenty animals."

The road wound along the edge of a steep valley and then led to a site of broken columns, a long-forgotten ruin from ancient times. "Look at the kites," Xeena said, pointing out a pair of large black birds perched like shadowy sentries atop the remains of a stone wall.

Alec watched the scenery sleepily and was starting to drift off when the convoy stopped to get coffee and fuel and to check their gear. As Karst mingled with the rest of the crew, Alec tended to the Black. The stallion was a good traveler when he wanted to be and dozed quietly in the back of the van. Alec adjusted the stable blanket, which was slipping off on one side.

Xeena came around to the rear of the van and peeked over the open half doors.

"Everything okay?" she asked.

"Shhh," Alec said, pressing a finger to his lips. He quietly slipped out of the Black's stall.

"He's sleeping?" she asked. Alec nodded. Xeena handed him a can of soda. "I thought you might be thirsty," she said.

Over by the cafeteria truck, the voices of the crew rose and fell, laughing, arguing, English mixed with Greek, German, Italian and languages Alec didn't recognize at all. Alec and Xeena sat on a picnic table at the edge of the parking lot.

"So tell me your story, Xeena," Alec said. "I really don't know much about your family except that you come from Xanthi. That and you are all pretty good riders."

"Thanks," Xeena said. "That means a lot coming from you."

"Xanthi seems like a nice place," Alec said. "Has your family always lived there?"

"For a long time. Why?"

"You just seem different than the others."

"What do you mean?"

Alec fumbled for an explanation. "I don't know. There is just something in the way you all carry yourselves, your expressions. It is as if nothing could surprise you."

"We are Thracian," Xeena said. "This land is our home. Our ancestors came from Acracia. Only full-blooded Thracians lived there."

"Acracia?" Alec asked. "Isn't that where we're going now?"

"We're going to the monastery," Xeena said. "The village of Acracia no longer exists. Even when it did, it was small and hard to find, or so the old folks say. It wasn't even on most maps."

"What happened to it?" Alec asked.

Xeena shrugged. "Mom's family left a long time ago. My grandfather Popi was born there, but his family left soon after."

"Why?"

"The goats weren't giving milk. The sheep were dying. Some said it had to do with the water, something about a small, illegal mine that polluted the river upstream. No one really knows the truth. I don't think there is anything wrong with the water anymore, though. The last I heard, the place had been turned into some super-exclusive health resort."

"Have you ever been there?" Alec asked.

"To the resort?" Xeena said. "No."

"You live this close and you have never been there? Why not?"

"Access to the resort is even more restrictive than to the monastery," she said. "The monastery is in the forest reserve on the other side of the mountain. No one I know, or ever heard of, has been to the resort part of the mountain where my grandfather's village used to be."

"Sounds mysterious," Alec said.

"It is," Xeena said. "My cousin tried to get a job there once, but it turned out that all the workers at the resort come from faraway places in Asia. They live on the premises and don't go to town. All supplies are delivered by their own trucks. Someone else said the resort isn't even in business anymore, but no one seems to know for sure. As for my grandfather's village, all that is left are stories."

Karst came around the side of the van and called Xeena over. He spoke to his daughter in rapid Greek. Xeena hurried over to one of the horse vans parked beside them.

"Hokay, Alec," he said, "We go now. Xeena go with other van. You go with me."

Alec did another quick check on the Black and made sure everything in the back of the van was secure and in order. Then he closed the rear half doors and swung up into his seat in the van with Karst.

"Xeena ride with Thomas," the trainer said. "Some his horses, uh . . . not quiet. She help."

The convoy started off again, and soon they were crawling up the switchback road. Alec saw that there was more light in the sky now, the sun bringing warmth into the day.

A tour bus pulled beside them on a straightaway, honking its horn and barreling ahead. Karst made a hand gesture out the window and grumbled an oath in Greek. The bus sent a cloud of dust pouring over them as it roared by. Other than that, there was little traffic, though at one point a line of shiny black Mercedeses with darkened windows flew by in the other direction. "Government cars," Karst said with a laugh. "Big bosses."

In a few minutes, they were surrounded by woods once more. Vast trees on either side interlocked their leafy, moss-covered branches above them. Alec gazed through the windshield at the tunnel of trees and the darker shadows of the woods beyond. Ghostly vapors and traces of mist hung low to the ground in small clearings. Spears of sunlight streaked down through the swaying treetops and flickered on the road ahead. He could hear birdsongs, and the wind coming through the open window carried the scent of forest flowers.

Karst leaned his head out the window and drew in a great breath of air and let it out. "Air nice here," he said. "Mountains make clean. Clear. All the time nice, a' clear."

For many miles, the convoy passed in and out of tree tunnels and through more forest groves and rock gardens. The road divided and a sign, written in Greek, German, English and French, indicated the way to the scenic overlook in the forest reserve. Pointing the other way was another sign, lettered in a language that Alec couldn't read, perhaps Greek or Bulgarian. This was the direction they followed.

The twisting road rose and fell as the convoy made its way up the mountain. The curves were sharp, and in some places the van was forced to slow to a crawl to safely get around them. Alec looked at his watch and realized they had already been traveling for more than five hours.

Soon the road dipped again, running down to a fifty-foot-long wooden bridge that spanned a roiling white-water river. The convoy eased carefully over the bridge and after another mile came to a narrow lane leading off to the south. They turned onto the lane. It was a rougher ride, and the road was splotched in places with dried mud. After about a quarter mile, just over the crest of a hill, they saw the high walls of the monastery.

Two monks, with beards and clean-shaven heads

and wearing heavy robes belted by thick white ropes, were waiting for them at a gate barricading the driveway. After opening the gate, the taller of the two set off up the driveway on foot and gestured for the trucks to follow him.

The monk led them toward a compound of low stone buildings just outside the twenty-foot-high monastery walls. Alongside the outbuildings were rows of white tents set up around a spacious brick courtyard. Karst told Alec the tents had been prepared by a crew that came up last night and had been working all day to get everything ready for their arrival. Each tent served a different purpose. Some were stables for the animals, while others were wardrobe, makeup and dressing rooms for the actors.

The vans and equipment trucks crept ahead and then pulled over to the side of the drive. Alec looked over at the monastery, where he could see the castlelike tops of towers inside the fortified building. "Not bad for summer house," Karst joked. "We stay outside. Monks no like visitors."

Daylight hours were short here in the mountains, even in the summer. The sun was already dipping below the mountaintops by the time Alec had finished unloading the Black from the van and making the stallion comfortable in his tent.

The Black's tent was almost the size of a two-car garage, plenty big enough to accommodate the stallion and its other occupants, the pair of scruffy-looking white goats Alec had seen loading up earlier. The portable stalls inside the tent were made of iron bars, wood and plastic, and it amazed Alec how quickly the carpenters had been able to snap them together. The Black's box stall was large and roomy, with straw bedding covering the ground. There was a wide aisle that contained an area for Alec to keep the gear and supplies he'd brought with him: tack trunks, a couple sacks of feed, blankets, saddles and fold-up stable cots. The tent walls were pegged tight and weighted down with sandbags. Stabled in the next tent were the wranglers' riding ponies, including Cleo, Xeena's favorite. There was another tent for Tina and the other picture horses, and smaller tents for the weasels, snakes and ducks.

Beyond the row of animal tents, in a corner of the compound about forty yards away, the camera crew and other technicians were already busy blocking out a shot and setting up for the director's arrival by chopper the next day. Alec helped tend the other horses but mostly just kept an eye on the Black.

A production assistant showed Alec to his lodgings, a small corner room located in one of the larger outbuildings that surrounded the courtyard. There was a bed, a chair and a table on which sat a large empty bowl and a pitcher of water. The bathroom was down at the end of the hall.

Alec washed up and changed his shirt. There was no mirror in the bathroom, or in his room for that matter, and he wondered if maybe the monks didn't believe in them.

When it was time for dinner, Alec set off across the courtyard and past the outbuildings that were being used as housing for the production staff, actors and crew. The buildings appeared so similar that Alec wondered how he was ever going to find his way back to his own room again.

Soon he saw a group of people filing through the high, arched doorway of the building that was apparently serving as the crew's dining room. It didn't take long for him to realize that the building had been a large stable at one time, probably more than a century ago. Alec got a kick out of the thought that the crew had brought portable stables for the horses and other animals, and they were now going to be eating in the original stable.

The room was spacious enough for the fifty or sixty men and women gathered there. Tables and chairs were set up in rows to accommodate everyone. The food was tasty—meat, vegetables and soup, simple but plentiful—all supplied courtesy of the film producers and excellently prepared by the location catering staff.

Neither Karst nor Xeena were in the dining area, and Alec figured they must have eaten earlier. He found a place at a table with a pair of young women who turned out to be set carpenters from California. They talked about the ride up through the woods and the quality of the food, and they wondered about the mysterious inhabitants of the monastery. Alec looked around the room once again and could see no sign of the monks who lived in this place.

After dinner, he grabbed his flashlight and walked out to the stable area to check on the Black. He had already given the stallion his supper an hour earlier, a light meal of barley, hay and oats. Alec had brought feed with him all the way from Hopeful Farm, just to be safe.

Alec broke out a pair of soft brushes from the tack trunk and gave the Black a quick grooming for the fun of it. The stallion leaned into the brush strokes with pleasure, then grew impatient and stepped away.

"Had enough, eh?" Alec said. The Black tossed his head affirmatively. Alec smiled. "I know, I know. You want to get outside and do a little exploring. Well, you just have to wait until morning for that."

Alec shuffled his feet through the straw spread out on the floor of the Black's stall. "Look," he said. "It's not so bad here. All the nice bedding we brought in for you. Why, you're living like a king's horse. Like old Mister Bucephalus himself."

The Black turned to look out the tent entrance at the forest beyond. He pricked his ears and raised his head as if scenting something in the draft of wind leaking through the tent flaps, perhaps something not so far away. But soon the draft died and the stallion lost interest, switching his attention to the hay net hanging in the corner of his stall.

A few minutes later, Alec pocketed his flashlight and walked out to drink in the night and enjoy the great, sweet silence of the mountains. A light wind came from the direction of the monastery. It carried an odd scent with it, a smell he quickly realized must be incense burning in the monastery temple.

Above him, the stars sprinkled in the sky mixed easily with the few isolated specks of light coming from houses on a distant mountain. Against the cold, dark backdrop of trees, it was almost impossible to tell the difference between the house lights and the lower stars. His gaze shifted along the deep vista, back to Acracia and the mist-shrouded peaks of Mt. Atnos, where he could see no lights at all.

3

Diomedes

Alec didn't feel tired, so he decided to take a stroll and enjoy the night. Outside the tent, a few oil lamps hung from tree branches and cast a soft glow over the courtyard grounds. He followed a walkway through the yard to a grass path veering off into the woods. Wondering where it led, he flicked on his flashlight and angled the beam up the path. Suddenly the light blinked off. Alec gave the flashlight a shake, and it came back on again. He made a mental note to put in new batteries when he got back to his room. Without a dependable flashlight, it was hardly wise to go trailblazing. On the other hand, he was still feeling restless after the long ride here and figured the walk might do him some good. He followed the path a little farther as it wound through the woods.

After a minute, he noticed someone with a lantern standing in a clearing up ahead. He drew closer and saw it was Xeena. She seemed to be gazing wistfully up at the mountains and the site of her lost ancestral home, now sealed off from the rest of the world inside the confines of the exclusive Acracian resort.

Alec didn't want to startle her out here in the dark, so to make some noise, he began whistling. He also switched his flashlight on and off.

Xeena turned and waved. "Hey there," she called.

"Lovely night," Alec said. "Not too cold."

Soon they were both gazing up at the stars, trying to identify the different constellations.

"Do you believe in astrology, Alec?" Xeena said after a minute.

Alec shrugged. "There might be something to it, but personally, no, not really. I don't know much about it. Do you?"

"My grandfather used to say our destiny is written in the stars. Popi believed some people could read omens and see prophecy in the night sky. He told me that there is a long history of fortune-telling in these mountains—at least there used to be."

Alec was about to say something but Xeena cut him off. "And he wasn't some superstitious old fool either, just because he believed in astrology," Xeena said defensively.

"I wasn't going to say that," Alec said.

"Popi was smart. He had a gift with languages— learned to speak English on his own. He was the one who taught me. He was also a successful businessman, even though his family was poor when they came to the city. He worked hard, bought a restaurant, then another, then a house and an apartment building. When he disappeared, he was quite wealthy."

"He disappeared?"

Xeena nodded. "One day he just sold everything, emptied his bank account and vanished. The police don't know what happened to him. My father thinks some criminals may have tricked him out of his money and killed him."

"That's awful," Alec said.

"I like to think he just wanted to run off and live by himself, maybe on an island somewhere. He was that type of person. In some ways he never really liked the city, and after my grandmother died . . ." Her voice trailed off.

Alec gestured to the dark side of the mountain. "So nobody lives up there now, aside from the people in the resort?"

Xeena nodded. "It's always been sort of a touchy subject for our families," she said. "No one even talks about the village we came from anymore. What I've learned, I had to find out for myself. Popi used to tell stories about his village that he'd heard as a little boy, stories about a secret horse cult that lived in the forest since ancient times, a cult that worshiped the Thracian god king Diomedes at a secret temple hidden in the woods. Popi said they even claimed to guard the bloodline of a fabled breed of horse that counted Alexander's stallion Bucephalus among its own."

"I thought Diomedes was a hero in the *Iliad*," Alec said. "Or was it the *Odyssey*?"

Xeena shook her head. "That was another Diomedes," she said. "This Diomedes was anything but a hero."

Alec nodded. "I've heard about some of those horse cults living in other parts of Europe in olden times, horrible stories about horses being killed in ritual sacrifices to warriors and kings."

"It was the other way around here," Xeena said. "Here people weren't sacrificing horses to people. Here it was the people who were sacrificed to the horses."

"People being sacrificed to horses?" Alec said. "That's a new one on me."

"These weren't ordinary horses," she said. "You should brush up on your history, Alec. Haven't you ever heard of the labors of Hercules?"

"Sure," Alec said, "at least the one about Hercules cleaning out some king's stables."

Xeena laughed. "I guess that makes sense," she said. "Well, one of his other tasks was to rid the Thracian Bistones of four man-killing mares owned by the king there, horses so fierce they had to be tethered with chains because they could eat right through leather and rope."

"Sounds like a horse I knew once," Alec said.

"The king Diomedes who ruled the Bistones was a cruel demigod, a tyrant descended from Ares—the Greek god of war—and a mortal woman. Hercules captured the king's mares but not before they killed Hercules's friend Abderus, and Diomedes too. According to the myth, Hercules drove the four mares all the way back to Eurystheus, where they were reformed of their bad habits."

"All's well that ends well," Alec said lightly.

"But there is another version of the story," Xeena said, "in which the mares escaped and fled up Mt. Atnos where they were adopted by a tribe of Acracians who lived there."

"Amazing story," Alec said. "And a bit creepy too."

"This is Thrace," Xeena said. "The Greek gods who ruled here weren't all pious and perfect like in some other places. Ours were more like a big, squabbling family, with all the good and bad. They could be noble and kind, but also vain and jealous. They were always fighting among each other and always falling in love with mortals or tormenting them."

A thread of silver light streaked through the sky

and vanished a second later. "Look," Alec said, "there's a falling star. Make a wish."

Xeena stiffened. "I am almost fourteen, Alec," she said. "Wishes are for children."

Alec shook his head. "No, they're not," he said. "It's okay to dream."

"Not if it's an impossible dream." Her gaze returned to the dark side of the mountain.

"Sometimes we don't know what is possible and what isn't," Alec said. "Look at me and the Black. He's desert born, from Arabia. I'm from New York City. Who would have ever guessed that we would have found each other or that we would have lived the lives we have lived together? Things happen. Last month I never would have believed that tonight I would be on some far-off mountain staring up into a Thracian sky."

"To tell you the truth," Xeena said, "neither did I. I am just a kid from Xanthi who happens to know how to ride a little. And that is only because my dad had a job at the mayor's horse farm, and I had an opportunity the other kids didn't. The only people I've known in my life up to now are my family, some of the neighbors and the people I met in school. Now I am hanging out with famous guys like you, and getting paid to do it."

"You have skills, Xeena," Alec said. "You can ride well, and that's why you are here."

The girl's gaze returned to the dark side of the mountain. "That's kind of you to say," she said, and sighed. "It just feels funny to be this close to a place I've wondered about all my life and not be able to go there."

"Maybe you'll get there someday."

Xeena tried to laugh. "Sure. Maybe I'll win the lottery too."

Alec didn't understand Xeena's pessimism, especially at her age. "You never know," he said. "Somebody has to win. Anyhow, you can always dream."

Xeena shrugged. "My dad says you should always hope for the best but prepare for the worst. Maybe that's the difference between Thracians and Americans. Maybe we know a little more about how hard life can be than you Americans do."

"I wouldn't say that," Alec said with a smile. "Life can be hard anywhere."

They stood there a minute more and then walked back toward the monastery in a comfortable silence. "So you ready for tomorrow?" Alec asked.

"Sure. I am going to be in one of the riding scenes, dressed as a warrior."

"Sounds good," Alec said.

"Jeff told me that they will need every person here

who can sit a horse," Xeena said. They talked a little
more about the plan for tomorrow and then said their
good-nights.

Alec turned down the walkway leading to the
Black's tent. He checked on his horse one last time and
then, with a yawn, started toward his room and a well-
deserved rest. The beam from his flashlight swept up
and down the path as he walked along, trying to keep
from stumbling over the uneven brick paving.

Finding his way to his quarters, Alec stepped inside the arched doorway and down a short hallway.
The door to his corner room wasn't locked, and he
stepped inside the dark, shadowy interior.

At that exact moment, his flashlight blinked off
again. Alec slapped it against his thigh a couple times
to get it working again. As he did, he noticed an odd,
musty odor in the air, a smell that hadn't been there
when he left the room before.

The light snapped on again, and Alec quickly
realized that this wasn't his room at all. He must
have gotten turned around somehow and come to the
wrong place. This looked like some sort of exhibit
room. There were framed black-and-white photographs on the walls and broken pieces of statuary standing in the corners. Curiosity made him direct the beam
of light to a pair of long, low glass and wooden display
cases lining the walls on one side of the room.

Inside the cabinets were what looked at first like vases and broken pots. As he looked closer through the glass front of one of the cases, he realized that the shelves were laden not with relics but with human skulls and bones.

At first the sight of the old bones startled him, but then curiosity once again got the best of him, and he pointed the flashlight at the framed photographs on the wall. One showed a pair of monks holding shovels and standing in a garden. In a hole in the ground beside them were uncovered pieces of an ancient Greek statue.

Alec stepped over to a wooden bookcase, its top shelf lined with old hardcover volumes, all written in Bulgarian, Greek and German. On a lower shelf was a stack of dusty pamphlets. The paper was brown and brittle with age, probably dating to the mid-twentieth century. Like the books, most of the pamphlets were written in languages Alec couldn't read. Only one was in English. Glancing through it, he realized that at one time there must have been regular visitors to this monastery and that this room must have been some sort of historical archive for the place. Apparently the bones and other artifacts were relics the monks had discovered while gardening or digging foundations for new buildings.

The flashlight started flickering on and off again,

and he quickly left the room. He took the pamphlet with him, hoping no one would mind and figuring he could return it in the morning after he'd had a chance to read it.

Retracing his steps through the courtyard, Alec reached the place where the path divided and he had made a wrong turn, arriving at last at his own room. He lit the lamp and checked all around the room just to make sure that he was in the right place this time and that there weren't any skulls rolling around on the floor. The sight of those old bones in the glass cases still lingered in his mind, and he couldn't help but feel a little uneasy about it now. He doused his face with water from the pitcher on the table. Taking a chair, he picked up the pamphlet he'd borrowed from the visitors' room and began to read.

As he thumbed through the pages, much of them detailing the long history of the monastery and the austere life the monks led there, he found one section that caught his eye. It was a chapter on Diomedes, the Greek demigod Xeena had told him about earlier, and the significance he had to this region. According to one legend, the pamphlet said, the demigod had chosen the forests of Mt. Atnos as a sanctuary to rebuild his kingdom after his defeat at the hands of Hercules. Alec leaned back in his chair and read more about the mysterious Diomedes:

The true history of the tyrant Diomedes is lost in time, but there are many fanciful tales to be told of the horse master of Thrace that are little known to the world outside of Acracia. The accepted view of Diomedes is that this demigod was the caretaker of four flesh-eating mares bequeathed to him by his father, Ares, the Greek god of war. The mares lived a privileged life, sequestered in green pastures forbidden to all save the sacred mares themselves. Diomedes's neighbors avoided his kingdom entirely. If by chance a foolish wanderer trespassed onto his fields, drank the water from his wells, or ate the fruit of his orchards, the unfortunate traveler was quickly reduced to fodder for the tyrant's man-killing mares.

In those days, word of the infamous horrors to be found in the kingdom of Diomedes had spread far and wide, but so had tales of the tyrant's superior horsemanship. According to one Acracian legend dating back several millennia, a spy managed to steal training secrets from Diomedes and return with them to his home in the distant land of Sybaris, in what is

now southern Italy. Diomedes soon learned
of the spy's treachery, and the score was
settled when he dispatched a messenger to
the Crotons, neighbors and mortal enemies
of the Sybaris, and told them how their foes
could be defeated. The next time the two
armies met in battle, the Croton soldiers
prepared by plugging their horses' ears
with wax. Then they sounded their charge
by playing a tune Diomedes bade his
messenger teach them, a melody that the
king had stolen from Orpheus, god of music
and poetry. Upon hearing the enchanted
melody, the horses of the enemy cavalry
threw off their riders and began to dance to
a music they could not resist. The battle
ended in slaughter and the downfall of
Sybaris.

Diomedes's reign of terror finally came
to an end at the hands of Hercules, the
renowned hero of ancient Greek myth.
Hercules fought and overpowered the
demigod, casting him to the floor of an
arena where he was taken down and
devoured by his own mares. Some scholars
count this legend, the eighth labor of
Hercules, as one of the earliest examples of

an adage that lives on to this day: *The evil you create will one day come back to destroy you.*

That is the story that is told in books and accepted by the modern world. But some of the villagers who lived in the region surrounding Mt. Atnos told another version of the story. They believed a demigod such as Diomedes could never be killed, and local legend had it that Diomedes feigned his death and that he and his mares live on to this day, hidden in a secret city among the wandering trees of a magical forest. Today's scholars accept that these tall tales about Diomedes were concocted by the locals as a means to scare off neighboring villagers who might have been tempted to expand their territories into the lush woods and pastures of Acracia. The same could be said for the folklore about poisonous rivers and spring-fed pools that drove mad any animal that drank from it, including humans.

In more recent times, Acracia has remained a fairly autonomous region. Due to its remote location, it escaped much of the hardship inflicted on the rest of Thrace by a series of foreign invaders. The last of

*those invaders were the Turks, who took all
of Thrace in the fourteenth century and held
it until 1920 when . . .*

Alec read a little farther and then turned to the
back pages. There he found an illustration of a bearded
man with heavy-browed, scowling eyes. The caption
below it read, "Diomedes—horse master of Thrace."
Alec looked at the illustration a minute and then put
the pamphlet away. As macabre as it all sounded, there
was something fascinating about the story of Diomedes.
It was always helpful to learn something of a place's
local history, Alec thought, especially when you had
never been there before.

Taking off his clothes, Alec lay down and crawled
under the blankets. But sleep would not come, so he
got up again, put his clothes back on and returned
to the Black's tent stable to sleep on a cot outside the
stallion's stall. He wasn't frightened, really, just a little
unsettled by the bones in the exhibit room. When he
felt like that, it always made sense to stay close to
the Black.

4

On the Set

The golden light of dawn was already filling the tent as Alec sat up on his stable cot and threw off his blanket. Molded by years of farm and track routine, he usually slept well and awakened easily, confident and ready to face another day. But this morning he felt a bit anxious as he looked around at the unfamiliar surroundings.

Alec rubbed the sleep from his eyes and stood up. Outside he heard a thumping sound that he assumed was Bateman's helicopter flying in somewhere outside the compound. A minute later, the *chop-chop-chop* faded away as the craft took off and flew back down the mountain. What a way to travel, Alec thought.

The Black was awake, and Alec went to his horse and gave him his feed and some fresh water. The smell of brewing coffee drew him to a table in the courtyard. He had a cup and said good morning to the cast and crew gathered there.

After the Black finished eating, it was time for a light grooming before they headed over to the wardrobe tent. The Black needed to get outfitted for the scene they were shooting that morning.

Alec spent the next hour trying to get the Black to submit to wearing the costume for his Bucephalus stand-in scene. Though the breastplate, feathered headpiece and other armor was lightweight, it was still cumbersome, and the stallion plainly didn't understand why Alec was asking him to wear it. He wasn't a trained movie horse and had never been schooled in the particular skills necessary to play a part in a film.

The Black bucked and pawed and was generally uncooperative, but finally Alec managed to get his horse suited up and more or less ready for the shot. Or rather, ready to wait for the shot. Once again, Alec realized that in the world of movies, everything was about waiting. You always had to be ready when they said you had to be ready, but it also seemed you always had to wait because someone else wasn't ready, or because a light stand fell over, or because a cloud was blocking the sun or because of a million other mishaps that could delay the plans for the day. All the waiting around didn't really bother Alec that much. If his life at the racetrack had taught him anything, it was that it never paid to be in a hurry. At the track, winners waited and watched and didn't get impatient about circumstances beyond their control. Sometimes it just meant finding a relaxing way to fill up the time between races. It seemed much the same here, and Alec was thankful he had a good book to read.

Finally he got the word that the cameras were almost ready, and they wanted Alec and the Black on the set in ten minutes. Alec was already wearing his costume but ducked into the wardrobe tent for last-minute adjustments. Xeena waited outside with the Black. Two costume assistants helped Alec get his helmet on and double-checked the rest of his armor.

"You ready?" Xeena asked when Alec emerged.

Alec nodded. "As ready as I'll ever be."

They started off for the set. Alec gave his horse a pat on the neck. "I wish I could explain all of this to the Black," he said. "He must think I've gone crazy, asking him to wear this stuff."

Xeena laughed. "He looks great anyway. He'll look terrific with the mountains in the background."

The scene was being filmed only a couple minutes' walk away, on a low hill flanked by looming peaks just beyond the compound. Jeff met them there and ran over the setup with Alec one last time. "Alexander and Bucephalus are reuniting after being separated during a battle," Jeff said. "Your job is to stand on top of the hill and call the Black to you when Bateman gives the cue."

"Sounds simple enough," Alec said. "I just hope the Black will cooperate. Anyway, we'll do the best we can."

The set was crowded with clusters of camera people, electricians, lighting people and assistants directing sunlight with reflector boards. Soon the cameras were in position and the crew was ready.

Karst was waiting for them at the mark where the Black was to start from. Alec had decided the best way to ensure the stallion came to him when he was turned loose was to tempt him with food. For this Alec was using a fresh carrot and a Jonathan apple, a tangy-sweet variety that the Black usually couldn't resist. Alec held out his hand and let the Black sniff the apple and then backed away from the stallion, showing him the apple and calling to him. The Black pulled at his lead, but Karst, with a little help from Xeena, held the stallion still. Alec took his position about twenty yards away on top of the low hill.

"Action," Bateman commanded over the bullhorn.

Alec called to his horse again, and this time Karst turned the Black loose. The stallion started for Alec but then gave a shrill neigh and took off in another direction.

"Cut," called the director. "Do it again." Wranglers on horseback and assistants on foot waved down the stallion and turned him back.

"I better get him," Alec said. He jogged out to collect the Black and lead him to his start marker.

"Easy, fella," Alec said. This time he gave the Black a taste of apple and a piece of carrot. But after the cameras were readied and Alec again called to the stallion, once more the Black bolted for the sidelines and out of the shot. They tried again and again. It took five attempts before Alec could finally get the Black to come to him as the director wanted.

Xeena walked with Alec as he led the stallion back to his stall. "That was so embarrassing," Alec said. "It looked like I had zero control over my horse out there."

Xeena nodded. "All the animals have been acting up this morning," she said. "Even Cleo, and she never gets worked up about anything. Maybe there is something in the woods around here. There could be forest predators, a pack of wolves or mountain lions."

"Are there animals like that living here?" Alec asked.

"I didn't think so, but you never know."

Alec shook his head. "Let's not worry about that unless we have to."

"You're right," Xeena said. "Anyway, we have Conrad's snakes to protect us. They are starring in their big scene later today. It should be interesting."

❖ ❖ ❖

After lunch that afternoon, Alec was sitting with his horse when Xeena popped her head into the tent. "Hey there," she said. "What's up?"

"Just reading my book," Alec said. "How is it going on the set?"

"Pretty good. The snakes seem to be feeling a bit lazy, though. How's the Black?"

"He's okay now. I don't know what got into him before."

Xeena smiled and took a seat on a bale of hay. "It's been that sort of a day for everyone."

"You should have heard the goats in the next stall a few minutes ago, bleating like murder. Something sure had them stirred up." Alec shook his head. "So what's going on with Conrad's snakes?"

"Right now they think the reason the snakes are so sleepy is because the ground is too cold," Xeena said. "Conrad says they need to heat up the sand to get the snakes moving again. Everything is stopped until the crew can bury a sheet of metal in the ground underneath where the snakes will be filmed. Then they will use electricity to heat up the metal and the layer of sand above it, making it hot enough so the snakes will do something more than curl up and fall asleep. You should go check it out."

"Sure," Alec said. He glanced over his shoulder

to where the Black had his nose buried in his hay net. "And what about him?"

"I'll watch him. Don't worry."

"I don't know," Alec said. "He's quiet now but earlier he was really acting peculiar."

"He'll be all right," Xeena said.

Alec thought about it a minute. "Seriously?" he said. "You'll keep an eye on him? I would sort of like to see this."

"Sure," Xeena said. "Go ahead. They are set up just outside the compound. It's not far."

Alec walked to a table and picked up a small black two-way radio. "I'll take the walkie-talkie," he said. "Let me know if he starts acting up."

Xeena nodded. "We'll be fine. No matter what happens, the set is only a minute's walk. Don't worry."

Alec jogged to the gate and out to the set where the crew was shooting the snake scene. The cameras were set up to one side of a Plexiglas barrier. It looked like a clear windowpane and was about six feet high and twelve feet wide. Alec figured the crew had already installed the underground heating pad, because Conrad and one of the other snake wranglers were now raking smooth the ground on the other side of the glass. The rest of the crew waited behind the camera, milling around or checking their equipment. Alec spotted Karst and Jeff sitting on folding chairs beside stacks of black camera cases. They waved to Alec, and he jogged over to join them.

Karst glanced at the set and shook his head. "Snakes," he said. "Train horses is hard. Train snakes and a two-year-old boy? I think we stay here all day."

Jeff laughed. "Whatever else he is, Conrad is a good snake wrangler. If anyone can pull this off, he can."

"Who is in this scene besides the snakes?" Alec asked. "Before, you said it was a dream scene, right?"

Jeff pointed out Carla, the sixteen-year-old actress playing Alexander's mom in the scene. "Freddy Roth has an eye for talent and picked her up in Xanthi," Jeff said. "Never worked in films before. That's her mom, Veronica, standing next to her. The other woman is Helen, from wardrobe." The three women were riding herd on a two-year-old boy who was having the time of his life playing with a toy sword someone had given him and kicking the air with his feet.

"Mr. Kung Fu over there is Otto," Jeff said. "He'll be playing the Alexander-as-a-kid character in the snake scene. Helen is Otto's real mom. They are German expats, living in Xanthi. Helen works in the wardrobe department, and when Bateman saw Otto on the set one day, he thought the kid would be perfect for the dream scene and Helen agreed. I don't think she knew her son's costars were going to be a pair of snakes, though."

Jeff gestured to where the assistants were just finishing smoothing out the dirt in front of the glass. "It looks like they have the hot pad in place and are about ready." He glanced at Karst and they both stood up. "We better stick close in case we can help in some way. Come with us if you want, Alec," Jeff said. "Just remember to stay well behind the cameras when we get ready to roll."

A few minutes later, cameras, sound equipment and actors were all in their places. Conrad stood back to one side, holding his snake-wrangling tool—a four-foot-long wooden stick with a hooklike tip. Alec briefly stepped behind Bateman and the camera crew framing the shot. He could see that from this angle, the glass was nearly invisible.

Helen brought Otto to his mark only a foot or two away from the glass and less than three feet from the snakes curled up quietly on the other side of the barrier. Otto barely seemed to notice them and occupied himself with digging a hole in the dirt and letting the earth crumble beneath his fingers.

"That's perfect," Bateman said. "Terrific. Conrad, you ready?"

"More heat," Conrad called to his assistant working the controls of the hot pad. Soon the leopard snakes seemed to wake up from their nap. One slithered to the glass and tried to climb it. Conrad moved his wrangling tool and pulled the snake off the glass. Then he gave the other snake a prod with the stick to get him motivated.

The snakes turned their attention on each other, facing off, winding up in coils, one twitching the tip of his tail threateningly. "Ready, boss," Conrad called out. "Better go now."

"Action."

Helen called a signal to her son from where she was standing just offscreen. Otto reached up and touched the glass and, for what looked like the first time, noticed the snakes. His reaction was more curiosity than fear as he watched the two snakes getting riled up on the other side of the glass. Suddenly one of the snakes darted off and the other chased it, both streaking for the edge of the glass as if trying to slip around to the other side where Otto was still lolling about in the dirt.

"Stop," Helen called in English as she dashed onto the set and scooped up her son. Conrad and another wrangler chased after the two runaway snakes.

"Cut," called the director.

"No worries, folks. They're not poisonous," Conrad called out. "Just give me a minute here . . ."

Karst nudged Alec with his elbow. "What I tell you," he said with a laugh. "Train snakes? I hope boss knows what he's doing."

The snake wranglers corralled the snakes while Helen listened to Bateman telling her she had nothing to worry about and that her child was in no danger. In the end, Helen apologized for spoiling the shot.

As the crew set up for the next take, Alec began to wonder how the Black was doing. He looked at his watch and decided he'd better get back to the stable. This was a job for all of them, and Xeena probably had other things to do than babysit the Black while Alec hung around the set like a tourist.

That night at dinner, Alec heard the snake scene was finally completed successfully, and after the rest of the day's shooting for the black unit was finished, Bateman helicoptered back to the film's base camp farther down the mountain. The director was scheduled back the next morning to finish up the last few scenes of the monastery shoot with the black unit.

Alec spoke with Conrad and some of the other wranglers. Once again, all anyone could talk about was the trouble they had getting their animals to perform. If they weren't fast asleep and unwilling to wake up, they were trying to bust out of their cages and stalls and run off. Alec wondered about this. In a way it was a relief that the Black wasn't the only one that had acted up today. Conrad said he would be glad when this shoot was over and they could get back home.

5

The Falls

Alec slept on a stable cot in the Black's tent again that night. The next morning he woke late. The first thing he noticed was how unusually quiet it was outside. He hadn't heard a helicopter or even the sounds of the generators powering up at the location site. Alec wondered if Bateman was even here yet.

The Black was awake when Alec stepped into his stall to bring him his breakfast. Alec spoke to his horse as the Black paced around his stall, the stallion feigning indifference to him at first. After a few more turns around the stall, the Black finally allowed Alec to touch his neck, then dipped his head into the feed trough to sniff at the special mix of oats and bran mash Alec had prepared for him. "Good morning to you too," Alec said. He watched the Black another minute and then went outside to the craft-services table to get himself a cup of coffee and a banana.

"There you are," a voice called behind him as

Alec made a beeline for the coffee. He turned and saw it was Jeff. "I checked your room and you weren't there."

"I slept out here. It was nice."

Jeff nodded and smiled. "I wanted to tell you there's been a little change in plans. Bateman's chopper broke down, and they are waiting on a part. It will probably take the rest of the day to fix it. The word is that we should sit tight and wait."

Alec laughed. "Fine with me."

"If you want to join us, some of the guys will be playing a game of cards in the dining room after breakfast to kill some time."

"Thanks," Alec said, and followed Jeff toward the dining area, where an American-style breakfast buffet was set up.

When the meal was over, Alec bowed out of the card game and told Jeff he was going to take the Black for a walk.

"Just remember, the other side of the river is off-limits," Jeff said as Alec got up from the table. "The government guy made that really clear. It's some club or resort or something over there. Plenty to see on this side of the river, I imagine."

"We'll be careful," Alec said.

Alec wanted to give his horse a break today, so when he led the Black from his stall, the stallion wore no saddle or bridle, only a loose halter with a short lead shank attached. A horse like the Black would not tolerate too much tack strapped to his body day after day, just as there were times he would not tolerate too much attention from people, even Alec. One of the important lessons he had learned from his horse, and it was true of all free-thinking animals, including people, was that no matter how much you loved them, or they loved you, the trick to getting along was to know when to leave them alone.

Alec spoke gently to his horse while knotting his fingers in two fistfuls of black mane. "Okay, big guy," he said. "Easy now."

With two quick, springy steps, Alec swung his legs up, rolling through the air to land astride a full seventeen hands of horse. His legs closed about the Black, and everything instantly fell into place, like the start of a familiar conversation.

Alec rested his hands easily on his horse's neck. "Let's go," he said softly, touching a heel to the stallion's side. The Black responded willingly and they set off. Alec saw Xeena, Karst and one of the grooms talking together at the far end of the compound. Xeena noticed Alec and the Black and waved. He waved back.

Passing through the courtyard, Alec turned the Black onto a path through the woods. He settled back to enjoy the ride, listening to the steady rhythm of the Black's hooves on the ground.

The path they were following, really little more than a woodcutter's trail, led to the top of a low cliff above a rushing white-water river. It edged along between the trees and the rim of the cliff and quickly became rough going, even dangerous, with little more than a network of slippery roots for footing.

Alec looked out over the roiling water running fifteen feet below. He dismounted and thought about turning around but decided against it. The path had become so narrow that doing so would likely be even more dangerous. The Black pulled ahead on his lead line, curious about what was beyond the next bend in the trail.

The path turned away from the river and continued upward around masses of jagged rocks until finally arriving at a clearing on the top of a hill. Alec stopped to catch his breath and take in the view. Overhead the sun had fallen beneath the clouds.

Suddenly Alec heard someone calling his name from the direction he had just come. It was Xeena. She was riding Cleo, the laid-back stable pony that she'd brought from Xanthi.

The pony jogged into the clearing, and Xeena pulled her up a short distance away. She swung out of the saddle and landed lightly on the ground. The Black eyed the pony and gave a snort. Cleo bobbed her head lazily.

"Hey there," Alec called to Xeena. "What's up?"

"We came for a walk, like you," Xeena said. "We've been on your trail since you left the monastery."

The Black stamped the ground and tossed his head impatiently. His pricked ears tilted toward the path on the other side of the clearing.

"Easy, fella," Alec said softly. The Black stretched out his neck, pulling on the lead line. Alec moved closer to him and gave the stallion's neck a gentle pat.

"Jeff was saying parts of the forest are off-limits," Alec said after a minute.

"Just on the other side of river," Xeena said. "The resort owns that part."

Alec shrugged. "I guess we're okay here, then. Let's see what we can see."

They both mounted up. Alec nudged the Black ahead. Xeena and Cleo followed close behind. After a minute, they reached another overgrown path that obviously hadn't been traveled in years. "I wonder what's up this way?" Xeena said.

"I guess we'll have to find out," Alec replied.

Grass grew tall on this new trail, and towering trees quivered all around. The trilling of birds filled the air. The Black heard the songs, too, his head held high, ears pitching this way and that, nostrils scenting the wind.

Though still rough going, the path ahead became wide enough that they didn't need to walk in single file any longer. Xeena pulled Cleo up beside the Black as they came to a grove of cedars. Beyond the trees to the east they saw a waterfall pouring from a high cliff on the resort side of the swirling river. For some reason, the sound of the falling waters did not roar but hung almost softly in the air.

"I didn't know there was a waterfall here," Xeena said.

Alec nodded. "No one mentioned it to me either."

Accentuated by the misty vapor rising off the falls, there was a feeling of great age in the tranquil atmosphere, Alec thought, maybe even outside of time. Somehow it was almost frightening to think about the history of a place like this, and how old it really was.

"It is certainly beautiful," Alec said. He wondered aloud to Xeena about the ancients who had surely stood in this very spot and viewed this same misty scene before them now. "Do you ever think about things like that?" Alec asked her. "Here we are looking at the same scenery they did, in a place that probably hasn't changed much in thousands of years. I wonder if the ancient Greeks were like us or if they'd even recognize us as being like them."

"What do you mean?" Xeena said.

"Everything must have been so different back then," Alec said. "Could their world bear any resemblance to the world of today? Did they see as we see, feel as we feel, think as we think?"

Xeena shrugged. "Why wouldn't they?"

"I don't know," Alec said. "People are different wherever you go, I guess, even today. Back then it must have been . . . really different. You can almost feel it in the air here."

"Maybe we should tell Jeff about this place," Xeena said. "Maybe Bateman could shoot a scene up here."

Alec laughed. "Hard to imagine a camera crew following the route we just took," he said.

The stallion led them out of the grove and down to the river's edge. There the trail followed along the riverbank in the direction of the falls. A steep, rocky slope rose up beside the path to their left, and the river ran swift and narrow to their right. Across the river, only about fifty yards away, Alec could see nothing but thick woods.

He looked out at the water cascading down and exploding in the river below. For a moment he thought he saw something moving there, a flash of white against the black rocks and silver spray. "Hey," he said to Xeena. "What's that?"

"What?"

"I thought I saw something over there," Alec said. "Something big."

"Where?"

Alec pointed ahead. "There . . . across the river . . . in those rocks, right beside the falls."

"Where?" Xeena asked again.

"There it is again," Alec said, all his attention focused at the spot across the river.

Just then, the Black lowered his head, sniffing the ground. When he straightened up, he jerked his neck so suddenly that Alec was caught unprepared. The lead shank slipped from his fingers and ran through his left hand.

Alec immediately moved to his horse, but it was too late. The stallion whirled and ran, gaining full stride almost immediately, his mane and tail streaming in the wind he created, the shank trailing at his side. In a matter of seconds, the stallion was fifty yards away.

"Black!" Alec called after his horse, chiding himself for being caught napping and losing his grip on the shank. Thankfully the stallion wouldn't get too far. The trail before him edged the bottom of the steep, rocky slope on one side with the river on the other. It came to a sudden stop about a hundred yards ahead where the path had been washed out by the river.

"Want me and Cleo to go get him?" Xeena asked.

"I better do it," Alec said. "He must be in one of his moods." Alec shook his head and broke into a slow jog. "Crazy horse," he muttered to himself as he trotted along.

The stallion reached the washed-out section of the trail and stopped. "Black," Alec called to him, again not too worried that the Black was doing anything more than playing around.

Then suddenly, with a wild cry, the Black reared, standing straight up on his hind legs, a coal-black silhouette against the swirling waters of the river behind him. Alec heard the longing in the Black's cry and instantly knew there was only one thing that could cause his horse to act this way. And there she was, a fantastic-looking white mare standing to one side of the falls on the opposite bank. Her snow-white coat was so brilliant and pale it appeared almost pink. Strangest of all, her eyes were a dazzling red, almost like rubies. Alec had never seen an albino horse before, but obviously he was looking at one now. She was one of the most strikingly beautiful creatures he had ever seen—and the most unusual.

Alec burst into a sprint, his eyes fixed on the two

horses. The Black slammed his forehooves to the ground and repeated his fierce cry, hoping to attract the mare's attention. Across the river, the albino beauty ignored him, paying the giant black stallion no more attention than she would a braying mule.

In his frustration, the Black stomped and pawed the ground, dragging up great clods of grass and sending them flying out behind him. His cries instantly became more demanding, more a threat than a request. She finally raised her head to listen, and then, with a defiant scream and a flash of snow-white coat, she was gone, lost in the silver mist rising from the falls.

Running as fast as he could, Alec closed to within a few yards of his horse. He called out again, but he knew it was no use. The stallion was beyond listening to anyone now, even Alec. Pawing the ground and uttering one last cry, the Black plunged headlong over the embankment and splashed down into the river. Alec reached the river's edge just behind the stallion and, without even stopping to think, ran in after him.

The Black squealed wildly as he jumped through the shallows. Heedless of Alec's cries, the stallion thrashed his way toward the middle of the river, determined to cross it and reach the mare he'd seen on the opposite side.

"Black," Alec called again, scrambling through

the hip-deep water. The tug of the current rushing downstream from the falls pulled on his legs. The river was little more than twenty feet from one side to the other, but it looked to be deep in the middle. Alec watched as the Black was swept into the deeper water and began to swim.

Alec waded out into the river, making for a shallow place he thought might be easier to cross. Suddenly his foot slipped and he lost his balance, sprawling face-first into the water. Instantly he was moving, caught in a rushing channel that was so deep he could no longer touch bottom. "Black," he cried, thrusting his head out of the water and twisting his neck around, looking for his horse but not seeing him.

Suddenly Alec felt himself reeling and rolling. The current pulled him below the surface. He came up for air and struggled in the whirling streams of water. His cold, wet clothes weighed him down, making every kick and stroke a double effort.

Battling the current was futile, so Alec let it pull him along, trying to keep his head out of the chilly water. He could hear Xeena calling and spun around to look behind him. She had followed him into the river and was standing in the shallows at the water's edge, waving her arms and pointing to the opposite side. Alec looked to where she was gesturing and saw the Black had already reached the other shore and was climbing up the riverbank. The stallion collected himself, clearing his nostrils and snorting explosively.

Floundering in midstream, Alec tried to call out to his horse but only managed to swallow a mouthful of river water. The water closed over him again as invisible hands seemed to drag him down to the bottom. His strong arms flayed the water as he tried to gain traction against the onslaught pulling him this way and that. Even his legs suddenly felt weak and useless as he beat lamely at the water. Finally he found the surface, gasping for air and coughing up water.

How could this be happening? Alec thought. Less than a moment ago, everything had been tranquil here. But now his heart throbbed wildly in his chest, and he felt consumed with a fear and desperation that came from something more than being separated from his horse and the beating he was receiving in the river.

Finally his feet touched bottom, and he clawed his way up the bank on the opposite side of the river, his body shaking with cold and fear and relief. He blinked his eyes, but the very air around him seemed clouded over by a great gray spiderweb.

Alec shook his head to try clearing his eyes and ears again. He heard the stallion's whistle, followed by a wild clamor of birds. Suddenly all sounds died away, everything becoming absolutely motionless and still, everything except the grinding of tree limbs whipped by a sudden wind and the soft murmuring of falling water. He could hear his own panting breath and could feel the thundering of his heart. Then there was something else, a girl's voice calling his name.

He blinked again and turned to see Xeena crawling out of the water and up onto the riverbank. She was soaked, her eyes large with fear and excitement.

"Xeena!" Alec said. "Are you okay? What are you doing here?"

"I wanted to help," she said.

"You could have drowned."

"You could have too."

"Yes, but . . ." Alec coughed and spat up some water. He shook his head once more to try to clear the water from his ears. "That river didn't look like much more than a gentle stream from the other side," he said, coughing again. "I feel like I just swam across the ocean. I must have swallowed a gallon of water."

"Me too," Xeena said.

Again Alec noticed the creaking of the windblown branches in the woods around them. All else was still. The silence seemed heavy, almost oppressive. "There's something really strange about this side of the river," he said. "I feel like I just landed on Mars. Do you notice it too?"

"I don't know," Xeena said. "My skin feels sort of tingly."

"Didn't you say there were old mines around here that polluted the water? Maybe that has something to do with it."

"Maybe," Xeena said. "Did you see that mare? Where did she come from?"

Alec shook his head. "Who knows? If we find her, I bet we'll find the Black, though. Let's go see if we can track them down before they get too far."

"He went that way," she said, pointing in the direction of the waterfall.

There was no path here, and after a few paces, Alec and Xeena had to stop to fight their way through head-high bushes and low-hanging branches. The wind whipped up again, turning the light greens to dark as it traveled through the treetops.

Finally there was space enough between the leaves that Alec could see where he was going. He slowed to a walk and wiped the sweat and water from his eyes. "Black," he called, his voice sounding hollow with exhaustion. The air around him was filled with a loud booming. What had once been the muffled sound of the falls had grown to a deafening howl on this side of the river.

"There he is," Xeena said.

Then Alec saw him too. The Black was storming toward the curtain of falling water pouring from the cliffs a hundred feet above. Alec could see some shadowy spaces between the rocks behind the falls, and it was there the stallion was headed. It looked to be the same spot where he had last seen the mare from across the river. Alec watched as his horse reached the falls and stepped into the shadows among the rocks. Then the Black seemed to disappear behind the curtain of falling water just as the mare had done earlier.

As the path cleared before him, Alec raced down to the edge of the falls. The mighty roar filled his ears and spray fogged his eyes. Wiping the water from his face, he ducked under a jutting shelf of granite.

Here was where the horses had gone, he realized. It was the dark mouth of a cave behind the falls, backlit by bluish sunlight shining in through the sheet of falling water.

Xeena came up fast behind him. "It's a cave," she said. "They went in here. Let's see where it goes."

Alec turned to the girl and shook his head. "I'll do it," he said. "You should stay here. I have enough to worry about right now without worrying about you on top of everything else."

"No way," Xeena said. "I haven't had this much fun in ages."

Alec looked at her and realized she was determined to stick by his side no matter what happened. There was no point in arguing.

"Okay then, but stay close," he said.

A three-foot-wide path rimmed the base of the cliff behind the falls, so smooth and flat it could have been man-made. Alec and Xeena edged their way forward, flattening their backs against the algae-slick rock wall as a rush of water flooded the path and lapped at their ankles. They reached the cave opening, and the noise from the falls howled through the air. Then they heard something else, a horse's scream, the scorching cry of the Black.

Alec stepped into the cave behind the curtain of falling water. He followed the sound of the Black's scream until he saw the stallion clambering across a streambed that ran behind the falls, water rushing high up around his legs.

The stallion whinnied again, and now Alec saw the albino mare standing like a statue, watching them from a ledge beside the far wall of the cave. She was gazing down upon them from the safety of the ledge, playfully tossing her head, her red eyes flashing like scarlet pinwheels. Alec called to his horse, but it was no use. The stallion was intent on reaching the ghostly vision of the white mare, and nothing was going to stop him.

The fast-flowing stream rushed by their feet as Alec and Xeena scrambled into the streambed and began wading through the water after the Black. The stream deepened, and too late Alec realized that the water churning around his legs here behind the falls was split into two opposing streams. The first was shallow and only reached his knees. It swept into the falls and down into the river outside. But the second stream looked deeper and ran in a different direction, inexplicably flowing back in the other direction, *back into the mountain*. Still Alec stumbled along, not knowing which he should fear more—being pulled into the falls or getting sucked deeper into the cave.

Swirling ribbons of roiling water tugged heavily at his legs. Trying to keep his balance was like trying to find footing on a slippery conveyer belt. Ahead he could see and hear the statuesque mare taunting the Black from her perch atop the far ledge.

The Black passed into the second stream and sank, the water covering his back. He gave a furious cry and half reared. Then Alec watched in horror as the stallion slipped and splashed down into the whirling water. "Black!" he screamed, his cry echoing down into the darkness that funneled back into the mountain. The stallion rolled in the water, then raised his head and whinnied again, a cry now filled with terror more than rage. His legs thrashed the water, but it was clear his hooves were no longer touching bottom.

Alec fought his way through the foaming stream, desperate to reach his horse.

"Be careful, Alec," Xeena cried out close be-hind him.

"Go get help," he called back over his shoulder.

The water deepened, rising past his waist to his chest. The current became stronger, like whirling chains tightening on his legs. Fierce and unstoppable the water ran, not toward the falls and the sun outside, but deeper into the darkness of the mountain. And it was taking the Black with it.

"Black!" Alec cried out again. Straining his eyes in the shadows, he could see his horse struggling against the current of dark, bubbling water that was dragging him downstream and toward the back of the cave.

For a moment, the stallion found enough footing to stop his thrashing and begin fighting the current. Alec splashed closer, coming almost near enough to touch the stallion. All at once, the Black slipped again and rolled into the water. Alec leaped through the air to make one last desperate attempt to reach his horse. His body flattened and was swept up in the turbulence, his hands stretched out.

The fingers of his right hand felt something and closed around the lead shank that trailed in the water at the stallion's side. With the touch of the rope came a feeling of intense relief. Whatever happened to them now, Alec thought, he wasn't letting go. Whatever happened now would happen to them together.

Alec clenched his fist around the shank as the current dragged them deeper into the tunnel. All around him was cold, wet darkness and black water. He saw nothing and heard only the slap of water on the walls of the cave. Alec quickly realized that fighting the rip current was harder now than before. Tied together with the Black, their speed was only increasing, their combined weight making it all the more impossible to battle the current. To make matters even worse, the water was deeper here, and when Alec tried to find the bottom, it was no longer there.

The rushing stream overwhelmed them, running ever faster as it hurried them through the lightless void. Alec fought to keep his head out of the water. All his channels of sense and reason seemed blocked, his brain racked by an overpowering fear. He felt more than heard a roar in the blackness ahead and around him, like the sound of an oncoming train inside a tunnel. The Black's lead shank suddenly jerked wildly and was torn from his hand. Alec grabbed desperately after it but felt nothing but empty space. The water beneath him fell away, and he was in a free fall, tumbling through a hole in the darkest night imaginable.

Alec had taken plenty of spills in his life, but never anything like this. "I am alive," he told himself, thinking of nothing else but those three words and repeating them over and over in his mind as he fell through the air. To black out now would mean to die. His only chance of survival was to stay awake and hope for a soft landing.

After a long drop, he hit the water again, water that felt like concrete as he slammed into it. Dark, cold wetness swallowed him as he was driven deep under the surface. Alec held his breath, hanging on to the three-word chant in his mind telling him he was alive, awake and conscious. He tried to roll himself into a ball and felt his body tossing head over heels until one leg struck bottom. It was a hard hit but not as hard as it might have been in shallower water. Pushing off the bottom, Alec swam for the surface, gasping for air as he finally reached it. Opening his eyes, he saw nothing. Everything around him remained pitch-black.

"Black," Alec screamed as he beat his arms against the current, groping the darkness, listening for any sign of his horse. He knew that if he had survived the fall, chances were the Black had too. And though he could see nothing in the darkness, he knew his horse must be close. He called again but still no answer came.

Alec realized he was now caught in still another underground river running somewhere deep inside the mountain. The current spun him around and dragged him along as he struggled to catch his breath. He commanded his mind to stay conscious. It was his choice to live or die, and he knew he must live.

For many moments, time seemed to stand still. At last he could see the tunnel ahead was no longer quite so dark. He began to make out the contours of the cave walls, twenty feet on either side of him, and the ceiling hanging less than six feet above.

The dark waters of the river funneled around a curve. Alec's legs bumped into rocks. His feet touched bottom, but he couldn't have stopped if he had wanted to. The current quickened as it approached a vertical slit in the dark rock wall.

The opening was a six-foot-wide gash in the rock and through it beamed brilliant shafts of sunlight. The current grew faster still, funneling water through the passageway and spilling Alec out into the blinding daylight. His eyes tried to adjust to the light as he was swept along in the ripping current.

At last he saw that he was now caught midstream in a river little more than thirty feet across, narrow and deep, almost like a canal. Bordering the riverbanks, tall, thick trees stood shoulder to shoulder.

As Alec gathered his wits, again his thoughts were for his horse. Was he still alive? Surely he must be, but where? And what about Xeena? Had she gone back for help, or had she been swept into the underground river too? He could only hope she had been smart enough not to follow him across the stream and was able to get to safety when she had the chance.

But there was no question about the Black, Alec thought. He must be around here somewhere, unless he had been swept down a different tunnel. Alec couldn't believe it. They had been only an arm's length apart when they dropped down into that hole or whatever it had been. Surely the current would have carried them to the same place. But where was that? Again his gaze searched the shore on either side, and again he saw wall-to-wall trees with no sign of anything familiar, or even man-made.

Alec raised his head out of the water. "Black," he called, his voice garbled and weak. He looked around him but could see no sign of his horse, only the monstrous tree trunks and the canopy of leaves above. He leaned back into the water and sidestroked along, edging toward the riverbank. Jolts of pain shot up his left leg as he kicked his feet. For the first time, Alec realized that he must have hit the bottom harder than he had thought.

The river hurried Alec downstream, curving around a bend. Using his good leg and cold, weary arms, he let the current carry him along until he reached the embankment at last. He caught hold of a tangled network of exposed roots beneath a tree trunk leaning over the river. With what seemed like all the strength he had left, Alec dragged himself out of the water and onto the bank. The ground here was all roots, thick and thin, layered on top of each other like a nest of snakes.

He coughed, gasped and cleared his mouth. He tried to speak, just to hear his own voice and confirm that he was indeed alive, but no words would come. He took a couple deep breaths and tried again, finally managing a low, guttural groan. Breathe, he told himself, just breathe. His eyes scanned the roiling water for the Black, but again he found no sign of his horse.

"Black," Alec called out, but he was so weakened by the ordeal that the sound of his cry did not travel far. If he could just find a path through the woods, Alec thought. If he could just . . . He tried to get up and then collapsed out of exhaustion, falling unconscious to the ground.

6

The Far Side
of the Mountain

Two hundred yards upstream, the Black scrambled
out of the water and onto a pocket of grass tucked into
the dense wall of trees lining the riverbank. The stallion dropped his head and stood still, thankful to feel
the earth beneath his hooves once again, his breath
coming hard and fast from his battle for life inside the
mountain. Maddened by the hellish experience, he
screamed an explosive neigh. His body was cut up,
bruised and beaten by river rocks, and chilled to the
bone by the cold water. And yet he was unafraid and
did not feel tired or weakened. Sharpened by his fight
for survival, his senses felt more acute than ever. He
wanted to run, but, hemmed in by trees, he was unsure where to go. Of one thing the stallion was certain:
He was in a strange new land, and instinct told him to
beware.

His pains were quickly forgotten as he stared out
to the woods and the peaks beyond, his small, fine

head raised high, sniffing the air, his nostrils quivering, his ears pointed and alert. Warmed by the sun, his body began to tremble, not from cold but from excitement and curiosity. The unknown woods, the strange path, the liberty to go where and when he pleased, all spoke to him of freedom. The sweet call to liberty was tempered only by one other thought— where was his friend, the boy who shared his life? He searched the air for some scent of him but could find none.

The stallion gazed out into the forest green and waited. Soon the breeze told him someone was there, or had been there not long ago. It was his own kind, of that he was certain, though there was something off about the scent, something unhealthy, the smell of fear and blood. The Black picked up the other horse's trail and before long found hoofprints and a mound of fresh manure. He kept going, wary but confident that whatever lay ahead, his speed, endurance and cunning would keep him safe.

The scent in the wind led to a narrow tree-lined path running away from the river. Soon the Black began climbing higher through the dense forest. The breeze softened, and as it did, the scent of horse became fainter and then vanished completely.

The stallion pawed the ground in frustration as it became clear he had lost the trail and was heading in the wrong direction. He listened and looked about him at the silent woods. Then, with a quick step back, he turned around and returned the way he had come, trusting his senses to lead him where he needed to go.

As the Black retraced his steps down the trail, he was again struck by something very strange. The tall, gnarled trees and piles of rocks that marked the path only minutes before seemed to have moved from one side of the trail to the other. His sense of direction seldom failed him, and the feeling of being disoriented now startled him. Other signs told him he had lost his way, signs he would have noticed had he passed along this path before. He sniffed the air, wary of this place where scents were so easily cleansed from the wind and landmarks seemed to shift and move around of their own accord.

Suddenly the trail opened to a clearing, one that hadn't been there on his way up the mountain path. His eyes remained sharp, his ears and nostrils alert, ready to catch the slightest noise or faintest scent. The sun shone brightly on a patch of inviting green grass. He waited until he was certain there was no sign of danger, then dropped his head to graze.

The sweet, clean grass gave the stallion new energy. Soon he felt enough at ease to lie down. He rolled on the warm ground and kicked his legs in the air. Climbing to his feet, he again whiffed a light gust of wind funneling through the trees. There was no sign of the mare, but once more the breeze carried with it the perfume of other horses.

He stood quietly, watchful and ready. The only thing about him that moved was his mane, stirred by the wind. Once more he felt the excitement of his new-found freedom in this untraveled land. Long-sleeping memories of life in the wild spoke to him as he looked around, memories of his birthplace in the high mountains of the great desert. Now he was free again, free to follow whatever path he chose.

After a minute, the Black struck out to chase the scent of horse, once again smelling the breeze. He found another trail and trotted easily through the woods, his hooves falling softly on the pine needles scattered over the ground. Winding his way through the trees, he lost the scent once more and was again unsure where to go. He stopped and waited to collect himself, listening for the slightest sound and puzzling over how to read the signs his senses told him were here. His powerful gaze searched through the woods. There was something out there, of that he was certain, but what?

The breeze stirred again and brought new information. He veered off the path and zigzagged through clusters of pines until he reached a place where the branches hung low, forming a tunnel of trees. The familiar scent of his kind became stronger here, and there were clear marks on the ground that others had passed this way not long ago.

The stallion moved slowly into the darker shadow of the passageway. Inside, the sound of the wind ceased. Strands of sunlight filtered through the leaves above and cast shifting patterns of light and shadows on the ground before him. After a few moments, the path opened upon a grassy pasture. The Black followed the scent upwind to a small stream. He stood still beside it, his nostrils flared, his ears cocked. There was a faint sound of splashing ahead, beyond a stand of trees.

Following the course of the stream through the trees, the stallion came upon a small pool. His eyes widened as he finally beheld what the signs in the wind had told him were there. It was four mares. Three were splashing about and playing in the water along the streambed. And grazing on the bank of the pool was the magnificent albino beauty he had first seen at the waterfall. She was big, lean but muscular, with a long, arched neck. Her head was small, her eyes large and wide-set. The Black stood silent and watched as the breeze riffled her high-set tail and the snow-white mane fringing her slender neck.

The albino sensed him well before the other mares. She suddenly became alert and raised her head

a notch. Then she froze, blades of grass still stuck between her lips, her thick forelock falling down to her
eyebrows. In the pool, the other mares were still unaware of the stallion's presence downwind. The albino
stared straight at the Black, but she did not cry out or
make any effort to warn her sisters of the stallion's
arrival.

The Black announced himself with a loud snort.
The mares in the pool stopped their playing and turned
to him. He remained still and watched them, dazzled
by their extreme loveliness. The band of mares looked
back at him, then at each other in amazement at the
sudden appearance of the stranger. With frightened
cries, the three ran from the pool into the woods, but
the albino remained.

The stallion waited, but she did not make a
move to follow the others. She was plainly unafraid
of the Black. Her tail swished angrily as she stared
back at this unwelcome intruder who had spoiled her
afternoon.

The Black stayed where he was. He knew that in
the wild, where there was a band of mares, there
would also be a stallion nearby. Moments later, the
band returned, but this time they were led by a young
stallion with a pale gray coat.

The Black whistled a warning and waited for the
inevitable. He felt no fear. His body began to tremble

in anticipation of the battle that was to come. It was not his first, and he knew what to expect. His courage and cunning would see him through this fight as they had many times before.

The young gray stallion screamed his challenge, throwing his head and tossing his mane. Then he broke into a run and charged to the pool, making a show of his speed and strength. The Black watched him, content to let the other stallion make the first move. The gray shrilled again, yet there was something uncertain in the sound of his cries. His long-limbed stride fell unsteady. The anxious gray broke his charge, slamming to a stop beside the mare on the far side of the stream leading to the pool. His red-rimmed eyes flashed and bulged in their sockets as he glared at the black stranger silently waiting for him.

All at once, the gray turned his attention to the albino mare, warning her of their danger with squeals and snorts. When she did not heed his commands, he swung his hindquarters around, lashing the air with his hooves. She sidestepped the blow, then with a savage cry, lifted her forefeet to trample the ground between them.

The enraged gray stallion whirled toward the Black and stood battle ready, his nostrils flared, his ears pinned against his head. There was no turning back for him now. Behind him, the band of mares clustered together for protection, watching and waiting for the fight to come.

The gray rocked back on his haunches and sprang forward. This time he leaped over the stream and made a headlong charge at the invader to his realm. The Black stepped forward to meet him, his fury mounting as he rose up on his hind legs, lashing the air with his hooves, then bringing them crashing to the ground. The lead shank dangling from his halter whipped snakelike around his head.

The two horses faced off for a brief moment, and the mountain air rang with their war cries. Then the young gray bravely reared and lunged at the larger, older stallion, his teeth seeking the Black's neck. But the gray was not quick enough, and one of the Black's forehooves caught him squarely in the shoulder. The blow staggered the young stallion. Moving steadily closer, the giant black horse took the offensive and rose up again, his ears pinned, his mane waving about his fine, small head like a black flag.

There were more squeals and the sounds of hooves battering flesh. Overpowering his attacker with cunning and experience, the black stallion landed blow after blow. And then the fight was decided, over almost as quickly as it started. The gray cried out in defeat and wheeled to get away. The Black chased him, but his intention was not to kill but only to frighten.

To kill one so young and inexperienced would prove nothing.

The gray scampered off across the pasture on the far side of the pool, calling for the mares to follow him as he fled. Frightened by the battle, the band had scattered but now regrouped to follow after their defeated leader. All but one.

The black stallion watched the mares run off and knew he could have taken them, but he let them go. He turned his attention to the one who remained. The one who had so captivated his imagination since he first saw her. The whitest of the white would now reckon with the blackest of the black. Surely she would accept him, even praise him in his triumph.

The mare stood in the streambed watching him approach, still unafraid, her ruby-tinted eyes holding him in their powerful gaze. Never had the stallion beheld such a horse. She was beautiful but somehow repulsive at the same time, unimaginably different from the rest of his kind. Almost imperceptible in the scent around her was something frightening, something that spoke of wolf or some other predator.

The Black slowed to stop and then stepped forward to meet her. She whinnied and tossed her head, as if to welcome him. Then, like a great white bird that had been driven from its perch, the mare spun around and bounded away. For a moment it looked as if she might turn back, but then she kept going. The stallion broke after her, but his hesitation had cost him. It would have been easy to catch her in the open, but the stallion knew that once she reached the trees, it would be different. This was her turf, not his. There among the unknown trails of this strange mountain forest, he would be at a disadvantage.

The mare reached the trees and slipped into the shadows. The Black raced in behind her. He had to slow almost to a stop to let his eyes adjust to the dark forest again. Even as he waited, the sound of the mare's hooves ahead told him where to go. Soon he was plunging through the mottled tunnel as fast as he dared.

He broke into a clearing again and searched for some sign of the mare. It was as if she had vanished completely. He frantically scented the wind for some hint as to where she had gone. Her scent was there, but his nostrils caught fresh smells, too, and his pricked ears could hear the sounds of voices, the sounds of people. The wind filled his nostrils again, and then, very clearly, he scented one person in particular, his partner, the boy who was his friend. With a fierce snort, he wheeled around to follow the trail upwind.

7

Acropolis

It was the sound of his horse's cry that brought Alec Ramsay back to consciousness. He lay on the muddy ground, trying to remember where he was and how he got there. Then came the whistle again, loud and clear, a sound unlike any other—the war cry of a stallion. It was the Black. Pulling himself to his feet, Alec followed the sound. The stallion was no more than fifty yards away, not in the water but already up on the riverbank. And he was not alone. A group of men were there, calling back and forth in excited cries and whoops. They wore white robed uniforms and carried pitchforks and spears. They were trying to surround the Black. The men closed in on the stallion like a pack of hungry wolves, threatening him with their weapons.

Who are these men? Alec thought. A hunting party from some mountain tribe? What were they trying to do to his horse?

Alec cried out but could produce only a strangled

gag from his water-tortured lungs. And, even though he was only a short distance away, the hooting men did not see him. All their attention was focused on the Black. Desperate to reach his horse, Alec took a step, only to fall as his injured left leg collapsed beneath him. He got up again and hopped ahead on his good leg. Each painful bounce shot an arrow of pain through his injured left ankle.

Calling out in words of some language Alec did not recognize, the robed men were attempting to maneuver the Black back against the stream. They formed a semicircle in front of the stallion, waving their spears and closing in tighter around him, blocking his escape.

The Black was standing his ground before his tormentors, rearing high, his forelegs striking out into the air. White lather ran in streaks across the glistening black satin of his shoulders. His mouth was open, his teeth bared. Lightning flashed from his eyes.

The men scattered out of the way as the stallion plunged his forelegs to the ground again and again, his body contorted, his eyes filled with hate. Thunder rolled from his hooves with each crash of his pounding legs. Then, with another wild, high-pitched whistle, he reared again.

One man strode forward, braver than the rest. He held a club like a baseball bat. When the stallion's hooves met the ground, the man lunged closer, fiercely swinging his bat.

With a quick side step, the Black avoided the blow. Reversing direction, he turned on his attacker. The man cried out as the stallion stuck him on the shoulder, butting him to the ground. The other men recoiled and then quickly regrouped. Brave in their anger now, they moved in to protect their fallen comrade, pushing the Black back against the stream. The stallion was trapped, magnificent in his savage fury, but also alone and frustrated.

Alec found his voice at last and called out, but the hunters were so caught up in the frenzy of their battle with the Black that they still didn't hear him. Or perhaps they did hear him but were simply ignoring him. Clearly the Black was giving them plenty to think about. Alec hobbled closer as one of the hunters pulled his wounded friend back.

Another hunter raised his spear, and at the same instant that Alec shouted "No," a cry cut through the air, an urgent voice calling out one of the few Greek words Alec actually understood.

"*Oh-hee!* No!"

It was a young woman's voice, and it startled all of them. The men turned in the direction of the shouts, and Alec saw the water-soaked figure of Xeena rush in to step between them and the Black.

More shouts filled the air as the Black noticed his friend. The men could not stop the Black as he broke away and ran to Alec.

Alec raised his arms to the stallion as his horse came to him. With the touch of his horse, Alec felt new strength pulse through his body. He rubbed his face against the wet warmth of the dark coat. The shaking and trembling of his body stopped.

They may not be safe, Alec thought, but they were together and alive.

Between the stallion and the sudden presence of the two waterlogged strangers, the men in the hunting party seemed unsure of what to do. One roared madly, another laughed, and yet another raised his spear and jabbed at the sky. Then, as one, they regrouped and turned their attention to the Black and the young man.

Xeena's voice rose louder. She was not pleading now. Alec did not understand the words, but the meaning was clear: stay away!

The men stopped. But then one stepped forward to confront the girl. Another shouted angrily to Alec in Greek, then in German and finally in English. "Papers!" he demanded.

The Black snorted and pulled back as the men gathered in front of them. Alec held on to the stallion's halter, feeling better for the first time in hours. After what had happened inside the mountain, this was nothing. Certainly the men would help them once they knew what he, Xeena and the Black had just been through. Up close, Alec saw that they all looked to be no more than teenagers. Their spears and white togas made him think of boys dressing up for a school play. But they weren't acting like boys. They were acting like police, and quite unfriendly police at that.

"American," Alec said, raising his hands. "Everything okay. No problemo."

The closest young man's face contorted with disdain at the sound of Alec's casual American voice. "Papers!" he repeated. It was an absurd request, considering the circumstances, like pulling a shipwrecked sailor from the sea and asking him for ID before giving him a cup of water to drink.

Alec patted the pockets of his soggy jeans and shrugged. "Sorry," he said coolly. "I must have left them in my other bathing suit." He wasn't used to being ordered about by a guy wearing a toga. He ignored the man and turned to Xeena. "Are you okay?"

She nodded.

"Tell these psychos that we need help, would you?"

"Papers!" the man barked again, shaking his spear for effect.

Alec was about to tell the man what he could do

with his papers when Xeena said something, and the man turned to glare at her, then pointed his spear off to the right toward the woods.

"Just do what they say, Alec," she said. "They must be the security force for the Acracia resort. They want us to come with them."

Two men walked in front of Xeena, Alec and the Black while the rest took up positions behind. The guards ushered Alec and Xeena to the head of a path leading into the forest. Alec kept a short hold on the Black's lead shank. The stallion had scratches and scrapes along his right side, but otherwise he seemed to have survived their ordeal in the underground river without serious injury. Of course, Alec would not know for certain until he had a chance to stop and examine his horse, and the guards didn't seem likely to agree to that. Alec could see they were still frightened of the Black, and they were dangerous in their fear. The one who had been knocked to the ground staggered along at the rear of the procession, his friends now leaving him to fend for himself.

The guards hurried them up the path, goading them along as if they were criminals. Alec limped ahead, shivering with cold. He was angry about the way they were being treated but smart enough to know that arguing was pointless. Sooner or later they would have to report to someone in authority. When they did, Alec planned on giving whoever it was an earful.

Xeena picked up a stick and handed it to Alec to use as a crutch. Alec started to say something, but she put a finger to her lips and made a sign to him to be quiet. Alec tried to read her expression. Somehow he wanted to laugh, just to break the tension. After all they'd just been through inside the mountain, now they were being hustled along by these spear-happy juvenile delinquents to who knew where? Alec shook his head. Whatever happened, he thought, at least he and the Black were on dry land.

Xeena marched along stoically beside him, her face a mask. What had happened to her in the underground river? Alec wondered. There would be time to talk about it later.

The men led them on, and soon the path opened up to a clearing bordered on one side by a stream and by woods on the other. This stream was narrower and slower moving than the one that had swept them through the mountain. The water was darker, too, almost black, even in the sunlight. Across the stream and beyond a narrow strip of carefully tended grass was a thirty-foot-high stone wall. The wall ran along in a straight line for what seemed a hundred yards or more in either direction before vanishing back into the forest shadows. Alec saw movement atop the wall, someone waving them all toward a heavy wooden gate. Above and beyond the walls were the tops of towers and temples. Some of the high roofs were curved like quarter moons.

What sort of place was this? Alec thought. If this was Acracia, it was supposed to be some sort of upscale resort. But the young men surrounding him didn't look like security guards to Alec. And why all the security, anyway? he wondered. Why the hostility? Didn't anyone see they were hurt and needed help?

The security guards drove Alec, Xeena and the Black forward. There was a small cabin next to the gate, a sentry post. A helmeted guard emerged, dressed in the same white toga-type costume as the others. He looked at them with suspicion. Suddenly everyone began speaking at once.

Again words flew back and forth between Xeena and the guards. Alec wished he knew more than half a dozen words of Greek; at least, he thought Greek was what they were speaking. Perhaps it was Bulgarian or Russian, but whatever it was, Xeena seemed to be holding her own in the conversation, her tone respectful but determined.

All at once, there was the sound of a horn trumpeting through the air. The guards instantly stopped their shouting. Standing at attention, they cast their eyes straight ahead. The sound from the horn faded, and a commanding voice called down from atop the ramparts. Alec looked to where the voice was coming from but couldn't see a thing.

Some guards remained at attention while three others ran to push open the heavy wooden doors. Here we go, Alec thought. At last they'd reached someone in charge. The guards backed off and gestured for them to pass through the gate.

The Black stood still, his head held high, his eyes peering beyond the giant, swinging doors, ready and alert for whatever might come. The stallion swished his tail lightly. Alec waited, knowing that his own frail, human senses could never match those of his horse. If there was danger ahead, the Black would be the first to warn them of it. Alec wondered what time it was. By the position of the sun overhead, he could tell they were already well into the afternoon.

Beyond the open gate were voices, but Alec could see no one. They started over a small wooden bridge, crossing above the stream and the embankment that edged the wall's foundation stones. The dark entrance through the gate yawned at them as they cautiously made their way past the towering wooden doors. The passageway led through thick stone blocks for at least twenty feet. Could these walls really be that thick? Alec wondered.

The passageway opened onto a path of hard-packed red dirt. Alec looked around him. At first he thought the place was a fortress, or perhaps a castle with a moat around it, the sort of place a medieval king might live in. But now he saw that the interior was much larger, a complete city surrounded by walls.

The dirt path ended at a stone block building. Atop the windowless structure was a balcony and beyond that a distant line of columns. A man wearing a sleeveless white tunic was descending steps from the balcony. A blue cloak was draped over his shoulder.

The man came toward them and called out in words Alec didn't understand. He was about Alec's size and young-looking, but his face was framed by a wispy beard. His hair was cut short, unlike the longer-haired security force from the forest and the helmeted guards at the gate.

Xeena returned the greeting, and they spoke a moment. The man kept his eyes fixed on the Black. The stallion threw back his head, and Alec spoke to him and held him still.

"What's he saying?" Alec asked Xeena.

"He says we must come in and that we are lucky to have found our way here."

Alec managed a laugh, gesturing to the troop of guards who had captured them. "I'd say we didn't have much choice in that."

The young man gave a small bow and spoke to Xeena, though clearly his words were meant for Alec as well. Xeena listened and then nodded. "He says we should follow him. He says we are just in time for dinner."

"Dinner?" Alec said. "Tell him we need a telephone."

Xeena relayed Alec's words, and the young man replied with a smile and gestured farther up the path. "He says he apologizes for the way we have been treated and that we should get some dry clothes and a moment's rest."

The robed man bowed again and then started up a path leading away from the balcony steps. Alec didn't have the energy to argue, even if he'd known what language to do it in. Alec, Xeena and the Black followed a path up into the walled city.

They came to a courtyard in front of what looked like a replica of a classic Greek temple, complete with high Ionic columns that rose to support a great gabled roof of carved stone. In the center of the courtyard was a small marble altar. A stone figure rose up behind the altar, a life-size statue of a rearing white horse.

It was an awesome sight, but Alec could hardly appreciate it. He staggered ahead, leaning on his tree-branch crutch for support with one hand and holding tight to the Black's lead with the other. Pain shot through his leg as he tried to keep up with his horse. He would have liked to mount up, just to take the pressure off his ankle, but he didn't dare risk it until he was certain the stallion was sound enough to handle his weight. After all they'd just been through, it seemed a miracle that any of them were still standing at all.

They crossed the courtyard, and their guide led them to a narrow ramp that ran up to the temple, a wide, empty pavilion with a stone floor and high ceiling supported by rows of columns. Passing outside again, they came to a plaza lush with grass and flowering trees.

Under one of the trees, they surprised three girls playing dominos around a stone table. All were wearing white tunics much like their guide's outfit. The girls had been laughing and talking but became quiet and stared as the strangers passed by. The guide greeted them, and the girls politely answered, then returned their attention to their game.

Alec looked around and was surprised to see so few people outside. The buildings bordering the plaza seemed almost empty, though he thought he could see figures moving within the shadows of the doors. But no one stood in their doorways or looked out their windows.

The Black nudged Alec's shoulder as their guide led them to a garden at the far end of the plaza. In the center of the garden, among the flowers and sculpted trees, was a circular fountain of marble and rough stone. On an island pedestal inside the fountain stood another statue of a rearing white horse, its forelegs striking out into the air. Like the statue in the gateway entrance, its neck was long and slender and arched to a small, refined head.

Someone was waiting for them beside the fountain, a short, bald man with a long, wispy beard. Despite the bald head and beard, he looked to be no more than thirty years old with a young face and sharp, deep-set eyes so bright and animal-like they were almost inhuman. He spoke to them in English with a heavy German accent.

"Welcome to the acropolis of Acracia and the palace of Governor Medio, a refuge from the modern world," the man said. "We have been expecting you, young Alex."

"Expecting me?" Alec said. "How's that? And . . . how did you know my name?"

"Could it be any other?" The man smiled and nodded knowingly, as if he and Alec shared some dark secret.

"Actually it's Alec, not Alex, but how . . ."

"Of course it is," he said, cutting off Alec's words. "Myself, I go by the name Spiro. There are few English speakers here, so the governor asked me to carry his blessings and bid you welcome. Acracia is honored to have you, young lord. Her cups are brimming over. May I offer you a drink?" He dipped a large clay cup into the water of the pool and held it out to Alec. "Drink deeply, and of your own free will," he said.

It was an almost ceremonial gesture. Even the cup seemed more like a chalice than a cup. It was hand-painted pottery decorated with horses, moons and stars.

Alec didn't want to be rude, so he accepted the cup and drank. The water tasted cool and clean, incredibly fresh. A tingling sensation warmed his insides. The man then refilled the cup and passed it to Xeena, who glanced at Alec and then drank from the cup as well. The Black sniffed at the water in the pool at the base of the fountain. He snorted, bobbed his head and back-stepped a few paces. "Easy boy," Alec said.

"What magnificence," Spiro exclaimed. "Is he of the red road or the white road?"

"Road?" Alec asked.

"Yes, by what path did he bring you here, the red or the white?"

Alec didn't know what to make of that question. He was cold and wet and had had just about enough of these toga-wearing fools for one afternoon.

"Path? We didn't take any path. We . . . But does it really matter now how we got here? We are tired. We are hurt. I need a telephone. We need—"

"All in good time, Herr Alex," Spiro said. "First you must get out of those wet clothes, have some food and be made comfortable." With a small bow, Spiro backed away and then gestured to the man who had guided them here. "Darius will show you to your quarters."

"Telephone," Alec said. "We need a telephone. Can't you find us a . . ."

Spiro gave no answer. He merely kept his head down in polite deference and continued backing away, then turned and walked off.

"What is it with these people?" Alec wondered aloud.

Xeena looked at him and shook her head. Her wet hair was plastered around her face and shoulders, her skin and clothes splashed with mud. Alec could only imagine how he looked to her.

He took a breath and shrugged. He'd been through so much in the past few hours that he didn't know what to think anymore. There didn't seem to be much else he could do but go along, at least for the moment.

Their guide gestured for them to follow. Alec turned to Xeena. "Tell him we need to get word back to the others about what happened. Surely they are missing us by now and wondering where we went."

Xeena spoke to the guide, and he replied in words

that the girl translated. "He says they will get a message back to the monastery for us. He says we need to come with him and that they have food for us."

"We need to get some food for my horse first," Alec said. "Ask him where the stable is."

Xeena translated Alec's question. The guide gestured to a grand-looking complex of buildings and replied. Alec could see Xeena was surprised at the answer. "He says the Black is coming into the citadel with us."

"Is there a stable there?"

Xeena nodded. "He says they have quarters for horses as well as guests inside. He says the Black is an honored guest, as are we, and deserves the finest accommodations they can provide."

"Guests?" Alec said. "But where in the heck are we, Xeena? Who are these people?"

"I do not have a clue," Xeena said. "The guide is speaking in Greek, but it's a dialect I never heard before. The one called Spiro who spoke English sounded German."

"But why the period clothes?" Alec said. "And these buildings . . . the temple columns, the statues and gardens. Who built them? It's like we just stepped back in time a couple thousand years. Is this a resort or some kind of theme park?"

Xeena shrugged, though her eyes were wide with

curiosity. "If it is the resort, I had no idea it looked anything like this."

Alec sighed. He was in a strange land, and his instincts told him to keep his head and wait and see what happened next before doing anything stupid that he might later regret. Maybe there was a phone in the citadel or wherever it was they were going.

Some food would be nice, Alec thought, again noticing the tingling sensation warming his insides. It was as if the water he'd just drank had been a super-fortified energy drink instead of spring water. He had to admit it was a good feeling, like a second wind, and he found new energy pulsing through his veins as they climbed another ramp. Even his injured ankle seemed to feel better now. Only minutes before, the aching pain had been bad enough to make his skin hurt. Now he felt as if someone were rubbing his leg with a silk cloth and soothing the pain away.

With the renewed strength of his second wind, Alec followed their guide toward a complex of simple, elegant buildings made of finely carved stone.

"That must be it," Xeena said. "The citadel."

Soon they were crossing the marble floor of a gallery. Two rows of columns, seven on each side, supported a double-vaulted ceiling. Stairways and ramps led up to the second story on each end. The ceiling was covered with glyphs and inscriptions written in a language Alec didn't recognize. A faint smell of incense tinged the air.

They turned down a hallway and came to a suite of apartments. Inside were spacious quarters that Darius indicated were accommodations for Alec, Xeena and the Black. There were three main rooms in all, one for Xeena, the middle room for the Black and the third for Alec. There were connecting doors between all the rooms and separate doors leading out to the hallway on one side and half doors to a shared balcony overlooking a plaza on the other side.

The Black's room was unlike any stable Alec had ever seen, more akin to the private sitting room of a wealthy English lord than a stable for a horse. Rich tapestries hung on the wall. The bedding covering the floor was not common straw but some kind of impossibly soft, gold-colored grass, like extra fine wheat or oats, with sweet-smelling white flower petals mixed in.

The Black whiffed at the bedding and then moved to a feed trough, which seemed to be made of ivory. The water pail hanging on the wall beside it was plated with gold.

Alec heard soft voices outside. A moment later, attendants appeared at the door like ghosts bearing gifts for the Black, soft wool blankets, fine brushes, a sponge, pails of fresh grain, almonds and raisins. Then, as quickly as they appeared, the attendants were gone again.

Alec sampled the Black's food before he gave it to his horse. The grain smelled and tasted a little sweet, but otherwise he couldn't detect anything wrong with it. The nuts and raisins seemed fine as well. This was something Alec would have done for his horse in any strange place they found themselves. There was always the possibility of the food being tainted or doped up. It only made sense to be especially cautious in a place like this, where he still felt more like a prisoner than a guest. The feed seemed safe enough, though, and Alec decided to give it a chance.

The Black set upon his food, and the guide beckoned to one of the rooms adjacent to the Black's quarters. Plates were spread out on a table along with bowls of grapes, bread, cheese and yogurt. There were towels and dry clothes folded neatly on an ornately framed bed. A steaming bath waited in a marble tub.

"You okay?" Alec asked Xeena.

"This place," she said. "I've never seen anything like it."

Darius gestured to the tub and spoke. "He says this is my room," Xeena said. "Yours is on the other side of the Black's."

"Sounds great," Alec said.

The girl nodded and gave Alec a soggy smile. They

hadn't had much to smile about in the last few hours, so it was nice to see. Darius spoke some words to Xeena, then bowed and began backing slowly toward the door. Xeena called a question after him, and he answered her in a soft, humble voice. Alec saw that she didn't seem satisfied with the answer and asked it again. Darius only repeated his answer, even more quiet this time. Then he bowed again, stepped out into the hallway and was gone.

Alec looked at Xeena. "What was that about?"

"I asked for a telephone," she said.

"What did he say?"

"It was hard to tell. The dialect he is speaking is very unusual, like I said; at least I've never heard it before. From what I can tell, he just keeps saying they will get the message out."

Alec shook his head. "Let's hope so." He looked down at the serving bowls and suddenly felt his appetite returning. "Come on," he said, picking up a piece of flat bread. "Let's eat."

After they finished a light meal, Alec stepped through the connecting door to the Black's stable, where he spent the next few minutes tending to his horse. First he led the stallion out onto the wide balcony overlooking a spacious courtyard. Alec found a bucket of hot water and set to work getting his horse cleaned up and dried off. As he worked, he realized that he had almost completely forgotten about his twisted ankle. It seemed to hurt hardly at all now. Maybe he hadn't injured it as badly as he thought.

His gaze stretched to the opposite end of the courtyard. Beyond a line of carefully trimmed trees, he could see a much larger building, like a palace, crowned with gables and royal-blue tile. It was rectangular and framed by a long row of columns. In front was a wide patio. Figures dressed in white climbed up and down the stone steps between the palace and a sculpture garden in the courtyard below. Around the courtyard were small buildings and guest wings, like the one where Alec was staying. Everything beyond was bordered by the high stone wall separating this place from the world outside.

Where were they? Alec wondered. It looked like some incredible lost city hidden from the world for centuries. Of course, it couldn't be that; it had to be some theme resort. Whatever it was, this place was unlike anything Alec had ever seen.

He rubbed down his horse with a soft cloth, the warm touch snapping him back to the present. There was a quiet alarm ringing in the back of his mind that told him to be careful and stay alert. Alec spoke to the Black in soothing words as he brushed the stallion's coat, drawing on the touch of his horse to give him strength.

After cleaning the stallion's feet with a hoof pick

that looked like it was gold-plated, Alec brought the Black back inside. The stallion seemed more curious than wary now. He nosed at the grain in his fancy ivory manger. Alec covered him with a stable blanket. It was made of a plush blue cloth, almost like velvet. As he pulled the blanket over the stallion's back, he saw an image woven into the fabric, a rearing white horse with a Greek inscription written beneath. The figure resembled the horse depicted in the statues he had seen earlier. Alec had also seen the image on banners that hung from some of the buildings they had passed.

Alec double-checked everything, then left his horse and crossed through the connecting door into his own room again.

He picked up the clothes that were laid out for him on the bed, a white tunic, a rope belt and a blue cloak, the same sort of getup everyone else seemed to be wearing. Leather sandals were placed neatly on the floor by the door.

Alec took off his wet clothes and stepped into the bath, wondering who had drawn it for him. There was an ornamented faucet plated in gold at one end of the tub. Fine copper piping etched with designs led from the faucet into the wall. Despite the ornamentation, the plumbing seemed primitive and not what a guest would expect in a first-class resort, Alec thought. The toilet was little more than a marble-lined hole in the floor. The room was lit by oil lamps hanging from the ceiling. He wondered if the people here even used electricity, as he hadn't seen anything electrical anywhere.

After a quick bath, Alec dressed and opened the door to the balcony. The terrace spanned the entire upper floor of the building, and Xeena was standing over by the edge. Like Alec, she had washed up and was now wearing the uniform of everyone he had seen so far in this place—a sleeveless white tunic tied at the waist by a blue cord.

She laughed when she saw Alec. "You look good in a dress," she said.

"At least it's dry," Alec said.

"How's your boy?" Xeena asked, and then followed Alec to the stallion's room to see for herself. The Black lifted his head from the ivory feed trough for a moment as they stepped inside. He came to Alec and eyed the girl briefly, then gazed out to the courtyard and the mountains beyond.

Alec glanced at Xeena and smiled. Gradually it seemed that the beginning of a friendship was growing between Xeena and the Black, Alec noticed. He didn't pull away from her anymore when she approached, and he even let her stroke his neck from time to time.

Alec pointed at the Black's gold-plated bucket. "Did you see that? It looks like gold."

"Looks like it."

"Same with the hoof pick."

Xeena shook her head. "Could it be real?"

"To be honest, I have no idea what real gold looks like," Alec said.

The Black snorted and Alec moved to his horse. "And did you see this blanket?" he said. "It feels like velvet. What's that say there? Isn't that in Greek? Or is it Russian?"

"It's Greek," Xeena said. "Old Greek. The classical kind that no one uses anymore." She read the words sewn into the blanket. "I think it says, 'House of the White Horse, particularly beloved of the gods.'"

"The gods?" Alec said. "Like the Greek gods?"

"Who else could it be?" she said. "It looks like whoever runs this place is trying to re-create a classical Greek city."

"They certainly have the money to spend," Alec said, "way beyond anything I've ever seen. I mean, who can afford a golden hoof pick?" He glanced at the Black and the white horse figure sewn into the blanket. "Any idea who this horse is supposed to be?"

"It might be Poseidon. He was the god of horses for the Greeks."

"I thought he was the sea god," Alec said.

"The god of horses too," Xeena said. "But there were other horse gods and demigods, too, like Pegasus.

Zeus supposedly gave Achilles an immortal horse—I forget its name—and there were other horse-type creatures besides immortal horses too. Some of them weren't always so friendly, like the centaurs that would get drunk on wine, crash wedding parties and carry off the brides."

Alec took a deep breath and looked at his horse. They had to get out of this place. The Black needed to get checked out by a vet. He looked at Xeena. "You sure you're okay? We're lucky to be alive after getting dragged into that underground river."

"I don't know if it's shock or what, but I feel pretty good now."

"So do I," Alec said, "but don't ask me why. My leg doesn't even hurt anymore." He shook his head. "But we still need to get word back to the others. And I haven't seen a sign of a telephone or anything electrical since we've been here."

"No mirrors either," Xeena said, "at least not in my room." They both returned to the balcony and gazed over the wide plaza, which was completely empty except for a few distant figures, perhaps gardeners pruning a tree.

What sort of place had they stumbled into? Alec wondered again. For the first time, the thought struck him that perhaps this wasn't a resort at all, that it was something else, someplace that really did belong to another time, a real-life Shangri-la. Who could say where that underground river had swept them to? Maybe, like Dorothy in the *Wizard of Oz*, they really weren't in Kansas anymore.

8

Fire-eyes

There was a soft knock at Alec's door, and he and Xeena stepped inside the room to see who was there. At the door were four attendants, young women in white tunics. They entered the room bearing vases of long-stemmed white flowers. With small steps, they brought the flowers to a table, eyes downcast, silent, with heads bent low deferentially.

Xeena spoke to the girls in Greek, then in what sounded like Italian. They looked at each other, and Alec thought he saw the glint of recognition in one girl's eyes before she averted her gaze and her face became sullen and empty again. Whether she understood and didn't want to answer or really didn't understand what Xeena was asking her, the girl only smiled and shrugged. Then the mute attendants set the vases down and left the room as silently as they had come.

A white envelope accompanied the gift of flowers. Inside was a note written in formal-looking English script. Alec picked up the note and showed it to Xeena. She read it aloud. " 'Medio bids you welcome and requests your presence at a banquet to celebrate the coming of the full moon. Spiro.' "

Alec couldn't believe it. "A banquet? After everything we've been through, we're supposed to get dressed up and go out on the town? This is just too much."

Xeena shrugged stoically, as if nothing could surprise her anymore.

Alec paced the room a minute, trying to collect his senses. What a day it had been, he thought. So much had happened already it made his head spin just to think about it all. He pondered the possibility of slipping out on his own and trying to find a phone somewhere but decided against it. He didn't feel comfortable leaving the Black just then, even with Xeena there. They didn't seem to be in any danger. In fact, they were being treated extremely well here, almost as if they really had been expected guests. Aside from the fact that there did not seem to be any phones, there was nothing to complain about, except . . .

Except there was tension looming in the air, and something told him to be careful, as if he, Xeena and the Black might have walked into an attractive trap. As it was, there wasn't much more he could do about it but sit tight and see what developed. And patience was something Alec was practiced at, a skill required every day at the track, especially at the jumbled start of a horse race. Somehow, at that moment, he could feel the same sense of anticipation, as if everything was about to bust loose. He told himself to be patient, watchful and ready to move when the time came.

A soft breeze blew across Alec's bare calves. He looked down at the sandals on his feet. He wished his jeans were dry so he could get out of this ridiculous outfit. It was like walking around in a knee-length T-shirt. He stepped over to where his pants were hanging on a chair and touched them. Still soaked. He felt the pockets and found a few coins inside one of them that had miraculously remained there through the ordeal in the river. They might be useful if he could find a pay phone somewhere. Meanwhile, he and Xeena passed some time pitching pennies against a wall while recounting to each other the events of this extremely strange day.

About a half hour later, Alec brought the Black out of his room and onto the balcony, letting him take a look around and scent the fresh breeze. The stallion peered out over the courtyard. His ears were pricked, his nostrils flared, his eyes alert. Alec watched his horse, and it gave him some comfort that the Black's light feed seemed to have agreed with him.

In the courtyard below, long shadows fell from the

towering colonnades of the palace and cast themselves in black bars over the steps. Farther back, beyond the environs of the acropolis and the high Acracian walls, the last flashing streams of late-afternoon sunlight purpled the mountain forest. Alec lifted his gaze to the horizon and the mountain peaks that rose up on all sides around them. A few specks of firelight twinkled like stars in the black night of the distant forest.

The breeze wafting in from the courtyard now brought with it the faint sounds of live music, the soft, faraway strains of a harp and flute. The music sounded off-key and ethereal, one more thing that seemed as if it belonged in another time. Alec looked in the direction the music was coming from and noticed the glowing of lights inside the palace. More people were gathering on the patio in front of the central building, on the steps and in the courtyard garden.

"Looks like something is going on over there, all right," Xeena said.

Before long, Alec heard steps coming down the hall, and there was another knock on the door. Xeena went to see who it was while Alec stayed on the balcony with the Black.

It was Darius, the guide who had led them to their quarters. Two attendants followed him into the room and out to the balcony. The Black turned his head and eyed the strangers suspiciously as they came closer.

Alec moved to his horse and put a hand on the stallion's halter. The attendants gazed up at the Black warily as Darius spoke with Xeena in Greek. Darius bowed and then beckoned for Alec and the others to come with him.

Xeena translated for Alec. "He says he will escort us to the megaron," she said. "I think that is what they call that large building. He says to bring the Black with us."

"Did he get in touch with your dad and the crew back at the monastery?"

"He says they sent a message."

"We don't need a go-between in this," Alec said, his frustration boiling over at last. "Where's the darn phone? I'd like to explain what happened in person. I also need to arrange to have the Black checked out by a vet when we get back. What am I supposed to do? Send smoke signals?"

Xeena relayed Alec's request to Darius, who only smiled, lowered his eyes and gestured to the hall door. The two attendants stood to one side, quietly waiting for the strangers and the giant black horse to pass. Alec hesitated.

Darius gestured again. "Come, please," he said.

Xeena looked at Alec. "Shall we?"

"Why not," he said. "Maybe we can find that

Spiro guy. I need to speak with someone in charge around here, someone who understands English."

Alec led the Black from the balcony and out to the hallway. They followed Darius down the hall to a ramp descending to the plaza below. The two silent attendants trailed behind them. Darius led them along a path of flat stone that cut through a lush lawn to the courtyard garden fronting the megaron. Young people were congregated there, including a group of women playing flutes and small, handheld harps. The music stopped and a hushed silence passed over the group as they turned their attention to the strangers and the magnificent black stallion.

The Black seemed to enjoy the notice he was getting, throwing out his forehooves, almost swaggering as he walked beside Alec and Xeena. His ears were pitched forward as he listened to every sound.

They climbed the stone ramp running through the center of the steps and up to the patio. As they reached the top level, the two attendants suddenly rushed up and stopped them before they could go any farther. Their quick movements startled the Black. He tossed his head and jerked on his lead line. Alec held the stallion tight while one of the attendants stepped over to him. The young man said something and touched Alec on the left shoulder.

"Hey," Alec said. "Back off."

The young man pulled back and lowered his head apologetically. Alec turned to Xeena. "What's this guy want?" Alec said.

Darius spoke up and said something that sounded like an apology. Xeena seemed to understand. She smiled and laughed.

"It's your cloak," she said. "It's supposed to hang over your left shoulder. I think it is some kind of protocol here in the megaron."

The attendant held up his hands politely to show he meant no harm. Alec fumbled with the cloak and then acquiesced to let the attendant pull it from his back, where Alec had been wearing it like a sloppy cape, and adjust it so it draped evenly over his left shoulder. The attendant gave Alec a courteous nod and stepped over to Xeena. She gave him her cloak, and he folded it carefully, then slung it over her left shoulder, fussing with it a moment until it hung evenly. When that was done, Darius gestured them ahead toward the torch-lit interior of the megaron.

Alec looked up at the Black and touched the stallion's well-groomed coat. Just pretend you're going to a costume party, Alec told himself. And however silly he might be dressed, at least his horse looked great.

They started down a long hall toward a wooden door. Decorative vases stood on the floor or on

pedestals. Much of the interior walls, cornices, panel-
ing and doors were painted in blue and gold. There
were few people here. The Black's hooves clicked
sharply in the quiet.

The big doors swung open from the inside as if by
magic, and Darius beckoned them ahead to a reception room. Tapestries decorated the wall, covered with
picture writing and strange symbols. There was a bust
of a young man's head on a pedestal, the stone painted
in flesh tones for the skin and red for the lips. From
the next room came the sound of a crowd.

They passed into the main room, where more statuary of ghostly white horses stood like sentries on either side of the door. A golden cage sat on a pedestal
of sculpted stone. Inside the cage, two blue birds trilled
a welcome.

The room was as big as a football field and lit by
thousands of candles burning in stands. At both ends
of the enormous room, logs blazed inside fireplaces the
size of small houses. Guests sat on the floor and at tables and on couches grouped around the three sides of
a long slab of raised marble laden with platters of
food. White-robed musicians strolled about playing
lilting tunes on harps and flutes.

"Look," Xeena said. "There are other horses
here."

It was true, Alec saw. On the other side of the

room, a chestnut Arabian mare stood beside a man re-
clining on a couch. A finely attired attendant carrying
a tray of food offered appetizers to the man and then
to the horse. Both declined.

Among the horses and people were three mares,
all colored a powdery white, all strikingly similar to
the albino mare he had seen at the waterfall that morning. These horses were not albinos, though. They
looked more like a cross between a Lipizzan and something else, maybe Arab, with dark eyes, fine heads and
short backs.

Perhaps he had been mistaken about the mare at
the waterfall being an albino, Alec thought. Maybe
it was one of these mares that had lured the Black
into the cave. Except for those red eyes—he certainly
couldn't have imagined those. And Xeena had seen
them too. No, Alec thought, that mare was not among
these three. Their coats were not the same impossibly
white color as the mare that had taunted the Black,
though they could have all been sisters they appeared
so incredibly alike. Their finely groomed coats shone
like pale sheets of smoked glass in the candlelight.

"People eat together with their horses in this
place?" Xeena said with surprise.

"I guess so," Alec said.

Well, Alec thought, maybe it wasn't all that
strange after all. He knew from firsthand experience

that Bedouins sometimes shared their tents with their horses. So did the Mongols and probably other people too. The big difference here was that this place looked like a king's palace, something far from a tent in the desert.

Darius directed them to one of the tables of honor near the long marble serving board. There were four finely carved wooden chairs with gold trim and gold velvet cushions, and there was plenty of room for the Black.

Alec stood beside his horse. The stallion was always unpredictable, but his years at the racetrack had instilled in him a high tolerance for crowds when necessary, and Alec was thankful for that now. The Black gazed around at the assembly, his eyes sparkling brightly. He was relaxed, Alec thought, and seemed to be enjoying all the attention he was receiving.

The guests' voices were a jarring mix of languages from all over Europe and beyond, from Russian, to German, to Greek, to Italian. Like the people, the dozen or so horses gathered in the hall were a mixed group, from enormous draft horses to elegant Arabs to tiny Shetland ponies. All seemed as at ease as the people in the luxurious surroundings of the banquet hall.

The aroma of spices and fine cooking filled the air. Xeena looked around the great hall, gaping at it all in openmouthed wonder, and Alec understood how she felt. It would have taken hours to ask about everything that caught his eye here. He lifted his gaze to the ceiling and saw murals depicting scenes out of mythology and a diagram of the orbits of the moon and seven planets.

At the sound of a gong, all the guests, horses and humans, took places at the dinner tables. The Black was served a bowl of fine oats that seemed ordinary enough to Alec when he gave them a taste test. Alec couldn't tell what the other horses were eating. The human guests were brought samplings of meat pastries and spiced vegetables. Alec and Xeena were tasting their appetizers when suddenly Spiro and a tall, blond woman arrived to take the empty chairs at their table.

"Mr. Spiro," Alec said casually. "Just the man I was hoping to see—"

Alec's words were cut off by the blare of trumpets, a fanfare to announce the arrival of the governor. Everyone stood up, and a man strode in leading a white horse by a golden rope. Instantly Alec recognized her as the albino mare they had seen at the waterfall. It seemed it had been a week ago but in truth had been only that morning. Behind the governor and the albino, a groom walked a young, gray stallion. He was of the same breed as the mares, seemingly similar in every way except for the color of his coat and his virile, masculine swagger. The gray pranced in proudly, then tossed his head and glared toward the Black's side of the room.

Alec had a hand on the Black's lead and quickly stepped up to his horse's head to keep him steady. But much to Alec's surprise, the stallion remained still, as if he was too mesmerized by the appearance of the ghostly albino mare to even notice the young stallion with her. The mare tossed her head but did not acknowledge the Black or the other guests.

The governor, the mare and the young stallion all took up places beside the three white mares at the center table. A hush fell over the assembly as the governor looked out among them like a king surveying his subjects. He was a big man with a soft, young face, almost like an overgrown baby, dressed in a velvet robe over a white tunic and wearing expensive-looking gold rings and bracelets. He addressed his guests in Greek and raised a goblet in the air. Everyone in the room stood up and raised their glasses as well. Attendants held bowls of water for the horses to share in the toast. The same attendant that had adjusted Alec's cloak approached the Black with a bowl, and Alec intercepted him before he came too close.

"Hold on just a second here, pal," Alec said as he took the bowl from the attendant and tasted the contents, just as he done with the Black's oats. It seemed to be nothing more than water.

A cry went up from the crowd. *"Chalazi to spiti tou Diomidi!"*

Alec glanced at Xeena. "It's a salute to the house of Diomedes," Xeena whispered.

Alec turned to see the governor on his feet and waving his cup. He was a giant of a man, easily six and a half feet tall, much taller than anyone else in the room, and yet his face was that of a child. *"Na Diomidi,"* the man called, gesturing to Alec's table and beckoning from across the room. All eyes moved to the strangers and the big black horse.

"He wants us to drink," Xeena whispered to Alec. "He's making a toast to Diomedes."

Alec raised his own glass and took a swallow. "I did," Alec said, holding up his glass and gesturing to the governor and his guests.

"I think he means the Black too," she said.

A murmur went up from the crowd, and some of the guests used their hands to pantomime lifting up a bowl and drinking. Alec looked out over the smiling, expectant faces at the tables around him. The governor raised his glass again. His gesture was more insistent this time.

The Black's bowl had been refilled. Alec sniffed at the water and tasted it once more. It looked clean and tasted fresh enough. He held the bowl so the Black could drink again. The stallion sniffed the water and took a sip. A roar went up from the crowd. Then the toasters sat down, and more trays were brought in. A moment later, everyone was once again merrily enjoying their food.

Spiro introduced the tall blond woman beside him as his wife. "Are you an American?" she asked in English, all smiles. Like Spiro, her accent sounded German. She had a boyish face with little blue eyes.

Alec nodded, then turned to Spiro and asked about making his phone call. Spiro told him that he had been in touch with the monastery and alerted them of their whereabouts. He promised to get Alec to a phone tomorrow morning, first thing. For now, Spiro said, Alec should relax and enjoy his food and the hospitality of Governor Medio.

Alec spoke, eager to share his thoughts with another English speaker. "What is this place?" he asked. "Where do these people come from?"

"All over the world," Spiro said.

"How do they find out about it? Do you advertise?"

"Acracia does not seek out patrons," Spiro said. "Word of its existence is known to but a few secret societies, the knowledge shared only when an initiate has reached a certain level of awareness."

"Why did those men attack us in the woods?" Alec asked.

"Strangers are not welcome here," Spiro explained.

"It is Medio's law. As his subjects, we are honored to do his bidding and pay him homage."

"Are you kidding me?" Alec said. "I thought this was a resort. And what do you mean 'we'? I am no one's subject. Who is this Medio person anyway? Can I talk with him?"

"You do not talk with that man; you listen to him." Spiro gestured out at the gathering. "He has brought us all this, and the waters of life."

"Waters of life?" Alec said. "What are you talking about? No one makes any sense around here."

"You cannot judge the governor as you would an ordinary man," Spiro continued, oblivious to Alec's comments. "The inexperienced cannot understand him. I am his chamberlain, and even I do not know him. Glory to the gods, we are all his vassals here."

Alec looked at Spiro's face. If the man is acting, he is doing a very good job, Alec thought. Plainly it didn't occur to Spiro that Governor Medio was no idol of Alec's.

"He lives here?"

"This is his home, though he retires to the shrine up on the mountain with his horses most of the year. These days he only returns to the acropolis for special occasions like tonight."

"He lives with his horses?"

Spiro pointed to the white mares at the head table.

"The sacred mares are normally sequestered atop Mt. Atnos," Spiro said, "at the temple of Diomedes. At this time of year, they sometimes come down to the palace for a visit during the full moon. Doubt me not when I say that it is with the mares' wondrous milk that the waters of Acracia are blessed, the reason the water here has such miraculous powers to restore vitality to all who drink it."

Alec started to laugh. "Is that what you people are selling here? The Fountain of Youth? I figured you were selling something."

Spiro lowered his head deferentially and spoke. "I beg your pardon, Herr Alex, but have I not heard that you were injured in some way before you arrived at the acropolis?"

Alec suddenly recalled his sprained ankle. He had forgotten completely about it.

"I grant you that it sounds mad," Spiro said, lifting his head and holding Alec's gaze, his eyes cold and sharp. "I would never have believed it myself before I came here from Berlin." His glare softened. He smiled and glanced at his wife. "I was a doctor there, a modern-minded man of science." Spiro sighed and took his wife's hand in his. "How life can change. This is our home now. Here we are among friends." He waved his hand to the other guests. "Could we ask for better company?"

Alec again looked over the people gathered in the banquet hall. It was true that everyone in the room appeared to be young, healthy and happy. In fact, there wasn't anyone here who was anything but young, healthy and happy. It didn't seem natural.

Spiro nodded across the room to the head table. "The White Ones are stabled in the finest quarters whenever they come to the megaron and are catered to like royalty," Spiro said. "She that stands to the governor's right is named Celera. Some call her Fire-eyes. She is Medio's favorite."

"Fine-looking animals," Alec said, glad to talk about something a little more down-to-earth.

"They are much more than that," Spiro said.

"Are they working horses?" Alec asked.

"Far from it," Spiro said. "The sacred mares live an easy existence in the woods and groves around the temple sanctuary. There they are pampered and live a pure life, free from any taint of earthly labor. Their only job is to be harnessed to a sacred chariot once a year or accompany Medio at court."

Another course was brought in then, skewers of meat, platters of finely chopped vegetables, bowls filled with delicate sauces. As the people ate, the musicians took up their harps, flutes and lyres again and began to play. A masked poet appeared and sang in Greek verse. Xeena leaned over and whispered to Alec that the poet was praising Medio's ancestors and insinuating they were connected to the gods. Xeena said he seemed to be making up the flattering verse as he went along, even suggesting the Black and Alec were connected to the gods as well.

After the poet was through singing, tables were moved and an area was cleared before the governor. Then a red carpet was spread out over the floor. An attendant walked the albino mare called Celera onto the center of the carpet. Alec leaned closer to the Black and put his hand on the stallion's neck.

The assembled guests grew quiet again as a veiled woman entered the room and moved ceremoniously toward Celera. The young woman walked with measured steps, draped in a cloak, treading proudly, deliberately, her head held high. Suddenly she opened her bare arms, threw them above her head and then swayed back and forth as though possessed by some uncontrollable desire to touch the ceiling.

The woman removed her headscarf, but her face remained veiled. Her raven-black hair fell down upon her bare shoulders. A man with red hair at the governor's table called out a question to her, and she laid her hands on Celera's neck. The mare shook her head and twitched an ear. The woman stepped back, staggering a bit, and then began speaking some words in a deep, sleepy-sounding voice.

"What is she saying?" Alec asked.

Spiro leaned forward. "This last part of the evening is for those who seek omens and monitions," he whispered. "The red-haired man asked the priestess, Cyrene, if the coming of the full moon tomorrow and the positions of the planets in the zodiac are an auspicious sign for him. The Oracle said that it was so."

"The Oracle?" Alec asked. "Is she an oracle?"

"The woman is only interpreting," Spiro said. "It is Celera who is speaking. Fire-eyes is the Oracle."

Other guests asked more questions, and the priestess interpreted the mare's murmurings and body language into words for the governor and his guests. For the next few minutes, the bizarre ceremony continued, the oracle Celera divining omens and dispensing advice to a half dozen different questions by way of her human interpreter.

At last the governor stood up and asked one final question.

"What is he saying?" Alec asked.

Xeena translated the Greek for Alec's benefit. "It's something about a messenger."

The priestess's deep voice uttered some more words. "My messenger is the message," Xeena interpreted. "The message my messenger brings is that the gods have sent Acracia a messenger."

Alec glanced at Spiro. The chamberlain said nothing, only watched him and smiled.

Alec looked at Xeena. "What's that mean?"

"I have no idea," she said.

The crowd took their eyes off Celera and once again turned their attention to Alec and the Black. Voices rose, and some guests stood and raised their glasses. The musicians suddenly redoubled their efforts. Drummers joined them and the tune became rhythmic and lively. People began singing. Medio left his place at the head of the table, and he and his entourage of horses joined Celera and the priestess on the floor.

The horses formed a small circle around Medio and pranced to the music, throwing out their hooves in short, mincing steps. They were quickly joined by other horses and guests. Soon the entire hall was filled with moving bodies, horses doing stylized leaps or skipping back and forth while the dinner guests spun and dodged between them like matadors in a bullring.

It was a scene out of a dream, Alec thought. All his senses told him to get out of there, but before he knew what was happening, he and the Black found themselves on the floor with the others, swept up in the carnival atmosphere. Alec didn't have much choice. There was no way out but through the crowd.

"Alec," he heard Xeena cry after him. "Wait."

Xeena caught up to them, and with the girl running interference, Alec did his best to guide the stallion to the exit, pushing his way through the dancing people and horses. The Black bucked around at Alec's side, trying to pull away, more playful than angry, enjoying the chaos and instability in the air. All around them were shouts, laughter, noise and the sounds of scuffling feet as people and horses jostled each other to squeeze into the crowd of dancing bodies.

In the middle of the room, the white mares were performing a finely choreographed dance that was central to the spectacle, occasionally springing into the air and twisting their bodies from side to side. The humans and other horses moved among them casually and with practiced skill. A deafening clamor filled the great hall, and the entire room seemed alive.

Alec looked about him as the horses became an incredible living carousel, a merry-go-round of real-life dancing horses circling faster and faster. Suddenly the music stopped and the carousel came to a screeching halt. Standing before the Black now was the young gray stallion, the one that had followed the governor and Celera into the room. A look of hate burned in his eyes.

The gray shrilled a challenge to the Black and deftly spun around, lashing out a hind hoof that just missed the Black's shoulder. "Whoa," Alec called out angrily as he hauled on the Black's lead. A gasp went up from the crowd. The uncontrolled gray turned again, reared and then brought his hooves crashing to the ground, as if daring the Black to step forward.

The Black strained to free himself and join the battle. Alec grasped the shank in his hand and threw all his weight downward, trying to turn the Black away and keep the stallion's hooves on the ground. Somehow he managed to hold the horse back.

Two men bravely dashed forward and got a grip on either side of the gray's halter, pulling the young stallion away. Then he was gone, lost in the crowd. As quickly as it had stopped, the music started again and once more the floor was a sea of people and horses meshing together.

Alec held tight to his horse's lead, but the Black seemed more shocked than angry now. What had happened to the gray? Alec thought. Then he heard a furious uproar coming from the other side of the crowded room and saw the young stallion, still bucking against his handlers defiantly. The Black saw the gray but did not make a move toward him, nor did he answer the cry of his attacker. Instead he twisted his head, unconcerned about the young stallion's threats, searching for someone else in the crowd, undoubtedly the albino mare Celera.

Alec felt someone tugging at his arm. It was

Xeena. "This way," she cried. Xeena pushed her way through the dancers. Alec pointed the Black in her direction and did his best to get the stallion to follow. A few of the revelers stared at the Black but otherwise went on with their celebrating, as if the confrontation between the two stallions was of no importance and best forgotten.

The crowd swallowed them up again. No one tried to stop them from leaving, but neither did they make much effort to stand clear. Xeena nudged, pushed and shoved people out of their way, and at last they burst through the swarm of revelers and into the reception room.

Alec stumbled ahead, keeping a firm grip on the Black's lead, still dazed by all he'd seen. They approached the exit, and the doors to the banquet hall opened as if by magic. The Black threw his head and cried out wildly as they passed through. Then the doors closed behind them and the clamor of the throng receded.

9

Dust to Dust

"How do we get out of here?" Alec said.

"I think it's this way," Xeena said, pointing down the corridor to the gallery they had passed on the way to the banquet room.

Alec kept a close hold on the Black's lead and spoke to his horse softly, trying to keep him settled. The words came in a steady stream that lasted until they had returned to the Black's room.

"What in the world kind of party was that?" Alec said to Xeena as he took off the Black's halter.

"Wild," Xeena said. "Really spectacular, except for when that crazy gray stallion went after the Black."

"He didn't concern me so much," Alec said. "The Black can handle himself with other stallions, and no one there seemed too surprised about what happened. I suppose that with all those horses and people bumping around together on the dance floor, a confrontation between horses wouldn't be unusual, no matter how well they are trained." Alec shook his head. "It's not the gray," he said. "It's that albino mare I'm thinking about. She's poison and the Black can't see it. If he gets another chance at her, I'm not sure I can keep them apart."

Alec walked through the passageway to his own room. He could see someone had been there while they'd been away. There were fresh blankets on his bed, and a fire had been lit in the corner fireplace. He splashed some water from a wash basin onto his face, then returned to the Black's quarters, picked up a brush and gave his horse a light grooming. The Black didn't need it, but the routine and familiar touch of his horse always made Alec feel better. Xeena stood at the connecting door, her eyes fixed on the stallion watching her.

"Pretty cool when you think about it," Xeena said after a minute.

Alec laughed. "Certainly unusual. That Medio really knows how to have a good time. Want to go back?"

"No thanks. I need to get some sleep now. But that was fun."

Could it all be just that? Alec thought. Just harmless fun? He had to admit that from the safety of his room, things suddenly started to look different. Could any of this be more than some kind of strange role-playing reenactment of ancient times, a place where people could get dressed up in costumes and pretend they were somewhere other than the modern world? He remembered hearing about people who reenacted famous Civil War battles in period uniforms. Maybe it was all just something like that. Some sort of club. Sure, Alec thought. That must be it. The only difference here was that these folks seemed extremely serious about it all, almost too serious, like actors who could not get out of character.

Perhaps he had overreacted, Alec thought. The gray was no threat to the Black. As for the albino, perhaps she was nothing more than a pretty white horse, a genetic oddity of nature on the outside but like any other horse inside. All the same, Alec still felt wary about everyone in this place, people and horses alike. There were no locks on the door, so he propped a chair against it for a barricade in case someone tried to slip into the room when he was asleep.

"If it wasn't night and I wasn't so tired, I'd say we should try to get out of here *now*," he said.

Xeena shivered. "I wouldn't want to go anywhere near that river tonight," she said.

Alec had to agree. He stepped into Xeena's room to help block her door with a chair, and then they said their good-nights. Alec returned to the Black for a minute and then went outside on the balcony. The megaron was aglow with amber light, and he could hear the sounds of the festivities continuing in full force. He sat down in a big, comfortable, wooden chair, leaned back and closed his eyes. Images from the day flashed through his memory: the waterfall, the albino mare, the swirling black water of the river, a sea of people and horses dancing together . . .

The world was certainly a funny place, he thought. And if these folks got their kicks out of dressing up and pretending to be ancient Greeks, who was he to judge them? Anyway, he'd be out of there in the morning. After checking on the Black one more time, he went back to his own room. Crawling into bed, he soon fell into a deep sleep.

The next morning, Alec was glad to see his jeans and shirt had dried by the fire so he could get out of his oversized T-shirt and put them on. Then he fed and tended his horse, just the same as he would have any morning anywhere. The sleep had done them both some good, Alec thought. The stallion leaned into Alec's brushstrokes with pleasure and shuffled his feet in the soft bedding, anxious to get outside.

"Okay, big guy," Alec said to his horse. "Just hang on a minute." He ran his hands over the Black's legs and was grateful to feel no excessive heat or swelling that might indicate an injury of some kind. It was truly amazing considering all they had been through the previous day. Even the scratches that raked his side seemed to be healing, almost as if they'd never been there.

Alec brought the Black out into the corridor and walked him up and down the length of the empty hall for ten minutes so he could stretch his legs. Then they returned to the Black's room.

Last night, Spiro had said he would get Alec to a telephone in the morning, so there was nothing to do but wait. The Black turned his attention to the feed in the ivory trough. Alec rattled around the room. Fifteen minutes passed, then a half hour, then an hour. He gave the Black another grooming and going-over with a rub rag just to pass the time.

The sun climbed higher over the mountain peaks, and there was still no sign of Spiro. Alec stepped out onto the balcony where Xeena was standing by the railing and looking out over the patios and gardens of the acropolis. No one seemed to be up and around anywhere. The place looked like a ghost town.

"I can't believe this," Alec said.

"I guess everyone is sleeping in after the big party last night," Xeena said.

Alec paced around on the balcony, waiting for a knock on the door. He was starting to get frustrated and wanted out of this madhouse. "Where in the heck is that Spiro guy?" Alec said. "It must be midmorning by now. He said he'd be here first thing."

"Maybe they reckon time differently here," Xeena said. "The monasteries do that. Morning to the monks is a completely different time than it is to people in the outside world. They use a different calendar too."

Alec looked out over the balcony railing to the megaron and the gardens and courtyard, the fountains and white statues. His gaze lifted to the ramparts beyond the gardens of the acropolis. High along one section of the fortified walls were figures moving about, perhaps lookouts or sentries of some sort. From the summit, one could probably see all around the acropolis, Alec thought. After a minute, he decided to go up there and take a look around. Even if he couldn't find a telephone, maybe he could get a lead on an exit out of this labyrinth. Alec told Xeena what he was doing and asked her to stay there and keep an eye on the Black while he slipped out to take a look around.

Soon Alec had wound his way through the maze of colonnades, patios and garden hedges to a walkway that led to the walls edging the acropolis. He'd seen no one along the way there, no sign of life at all except the trails of smoke drifting out of a few chimneys.

He followed the base of the wall until he came to a series of steps cut into the side and leading to the summit. He climbed the stairs to a narrow path of flat stones topping the barricade. If there had been anyone there before, they were gone now. All he could see were two small trees overhanging the railing, their white flower blossoms dangling in the branches.

Alec walked over to the trees, stopped and looked out over the mountains. From this vantage point, the walls looked as if they might encircle not just the city but also the entire top of the mountain. He saw a couple places where there were breaks in the wall, but only because cliffs and gorges made access impossible there.

Nothing seemed to be moving anywhere. The whole of nature seemed asleep—the woods silent, the sky empty of birds, no sign of life at all. He searched in vain for signs of commercial air traffic, or even Bateman's helicopter. Nothing. About the only movement he could see was a horse-drawn wagon on a road going up the mountain behind the acropolis. Alec wondered where it was going and if there were settlements closer to the summit.

Dark clouds were gathering around the mountain peaks, and it looked like a storm was approaching. A brisk breeze blew in suddenly, rattling the branches of the two trees beside him. Alec leaned over the edge of the wall as a white flower blossom fell from one of the trees and was swept away in the wind. He let his gaze follow the blossom as it twisted in the breeze and floated off. Then, as the blossom reached the other side of the stream beyond the wall, a peculiar thing happened. The flower seemed to vanish into thin air.

Alec blinked to clear his eyes and looked again. He picked up a fresh blossom from the ground and tossed it into the air. The wind caught the flower and carried it over the moat, and once again the flower disappeared, only this time Alec thought he could see a faint trail of dust falling through the air where the flower had been. He tried one more time and watched again as the soft white petals seem to dry up in midair, then crumble and dissolve to dust.

What could have caused that? he wondered. Was he still dreaming? Again he looked out to the world beyond the acropolis, his eyes searching for some sign of life in the forest. Where were the animals? He could see a few birds in the far distance but none close by. There were no squirrels in the trees, or on the opposite bank of the moat, or in the grass area bordering the woods. All of nature was fast asleep.

Strange, wild thoughts dashed through his mind. It was almost as if some invisible wall of death stood between Acracia and the outside world, a dead zone that drained away the life of whatever passed through it. Hadn't that pamphlet he read at the monastery said something about an enchanted forest that could hide whole cities and a poison river in the woods? And then there were those tall tales about the magical healing waters that Spiro had been going on about at dinner, waters blessed by mare's milk.

Waters of eternal life, winds of sudden death—could any of it be true? Alec knew that the stories were just crazy enough to be real. He had seen enough in his young life by now to know that most anything was possible. Understanding the how and why of it all was a different matter.

Alec retraced his steps to his room, determined now to forget everything else but getting the Black and Xeena and making a run for the main gate as soon as they could. From what he'd seen atop the barricade, that was the only certain way out of this madhouse. But when he reached his room, he found the Black alone. The girl was gone.

10

Forbidden Pastures

Alec checked the rooms, the balcony and out in the hall. "Xeena?" he called. "Where are you?" The Black was safe enough, but Xeena was nowhere to be seen. Surely she wouldn't have left the stallion alone unless it had been an emergency, Alec thought. He stepped out into the hall and looked up and down the corridor. "Xeena," he called again, and again no answer came.

Now what? Alec thought. Maybe she just went outside for a minute. He could wait here and hope she turned up. Or he could take the Black and try to find her. Alec moved to his horse. The Black was starting to get restless and pacing the luxurious confines of his room like a boxer gearing up for a big fight.

Alec looked out over the acropolis and the advancing storm clouds in the sky. After a minute, raindrops began to fall softly on the balcony. It would start raining now, he thought.

"Easy boy," he said as he pulled the halter over

the Black's ears and clipped on the lead line. Thunder rumbled and the pattering of raindrops quickened. He opened the big wooden door and walked the stallion out into the hall. Rain or no rain, there was no use hanging around here anymore. He had to find Xeena and get out of this place.

The Black's hooves clopped down the empty marble halls as they made their way to the entrance and the path to the grounds outside. The rain was falling harder now. Soon Alec saw a figure carrying an umbrella and approaching up the path from the other direction. The stallion tossed his head and gave a shrill warning cry. Alec tightened his grip on the lead and spoke to his horse to keep him calm.

The figure came closer, and Alec saw it was Spiro. "What are you doing out in the rain?" the bald-headed chamberlain asked. "I was just on my way to find you."

"I was waiting," Alec said, "but that doesn't matter now. Something has happened to Xeena. She's not in the room. She probably just went for a short walk and got caught in the rain or something but . . ."

"I just saw her a few minutes ago," Spiro said. "She was running up the road to Tarta."

"You did?" Alec said. "To where?"

"To Tarta. It is the next settlement up the hill."

"Why would she go there?"

"I believe she said something about her father," Spiro said, "seeing him in a wagon heading up the mountain. She wanted to catch up to him and would not stop to say more."

Karst? Alec wondered. What would Xeena's dad be doing here? Then he realized that Karst might have received the message about what had happened at the river and had come to get them. Either that or Karst had come here looking for them after they'd gone missing. Alec didn't trust the chamberlain, and there was no telling if Spiro really had sent the message last night as he said he had.

"Where is this Tarta place?" Alec asked. "Is it far?"

"Not too far," Spiro said. "But the girl will be fine, I am sure. Come. Let us breakfast together and wait for the rain to stop. Summer storms in the mountains aren't unusual. It should blow over momentarily."

Spiro gave Alec a kindly smile, but his animal eyes were cold and dark. The Black tugged on his lead, and Alec held him still. He shook his head. "Thanks, but I'd like to find Xeena. I know her father. Perhaps he came to take us back."

"Perhaps," Spiro said.

Alec again tried to read the man's expression but could see nothing there.

"Maybe that really was Xeena's dad she saw in the wagon," Alec said. "But maybe it wasn't. Either way I better go after her. How do I get to this place you say she was headed?"

"Follow the road up the mountain," Spiro said. "But you shouldn't worry yourself about the girl."

"I'll feel better if I know where she is," Alec said. "We've been through a lot since yesterday, and I feel responsible for getting her home safely."

Spiro bowed his head formally. "As you wish, Herr Alex." He pointed up the road behind him. "The turnoff to Tarta is no more than a couple kilometers. Bear left at the fork. But please remember to stay on the road. You will be passing through the pastures of the sacred mares. They are forbidden to all. You must not enter there."

Alec thanked Spiro for the help. He took hold of a hunk of black mane, stepped back and then vaulted onto the stallion's back. Following the road in the direction Spiro had indicated, they soon found the fork and headed left. Alec kept his horse to a steady walk. The Black seemed to be carrying his weight well. He moved easily beneath Alec, the rhythm of his steps even, his ears forward and alert.

The rain was slowing now, but Alec kept his head down and tucked his face into his horse's mane, letting the Black lead the way. Then, just as quickly as it had started, the rain shower stopped. A moment later the clouds parted and the sun was shining upon them.

Again Alec noticed the woods around him seemed to be completely void of animal life. It was unnatural, he thought. A place like this should be teeming with life, especially after a summer rain. The silence around him was unsettling as he recalled what he'd read about the poison river and remembered what he'd seen happen to the flower blossoms that had fallen from the top of the city wall. Some part of him just wanted to turn his horse around and get out of there right now. If it wasn't for Xeena . . . but he couldn't leave without her. Alec inhaled the smell of his horse. He would be all right, he knew. He was with the Black.

The road switched back and forth but remained fairly easy going for them at this pace. He saw no road signs, and if there had ever been any wagon tracks here, they had been washed away by the rain.

Alec wondered what time it was. Half the day was probably already gone, and the sun seemed to be getting lower in the sky. The Black raised his head and sniffed the wet air, then pawed the ground. "Easy, boy," Alec said, leaning forward and pressing his chest close to his horse's neck. "We'll get ourselves out of this place soon."

Around the next bend, the road ahead dipped and

entered a lush meadow with unfenced fields on either side of the road. These must be the sacred pastures, Alec thought, the place Spiro told him was off-limits. Alec had no intention of trespassing there whatsoever, though the pastures certainly did look inviting, with acres of green grass that ran all the way to the edge of the forest.

On the uphill side of the pasture, about fifty yards off the road to the right, Alec saw a small stream winding down from the mountain peaks. Beneath a towering oak on the other side of the stream were three horses. They looked to be the same mares he had seen the day before. They raised their heads and turned to watch Alec and the Black. One of them half reared and broke away from the others. She splashed through the stream and cantered across the field toward the road.

The Black stamped his forehooves suddenly. Alec pulled him to a stop. "Hold on, now," he spoke softly to his horse.

The mare ran up onto the road and careened to a stop in front of them, then stood there boldly, as if to block their path. Alec did his best to keep the stallion still. He could feel the Black tensing up, but only slightly, almost as if the sudden appearance of the mare was expected.

Alec spoke to the mare so she could hear his voice and know that there was no threat or fear in it. The mare whinnied and pawed the ground. The Black tossed his head in reply.

All at once, the mare began to move, stepping in place, then bobbing and weaving like a boxer, then prancing in a little circle, then backing up to pivot side to side in dressage-like movements. It was a display of true grace and beauty, a version of the same courtship dance Alec had seen at the banquet last night.

The Black seemed curious about the mare but also unmoved, or perhaps he was wary of her. She stopped dancing, then turned away and lowered her head submissively, now playing the shy coquette.

This was a distraction they didn't need right now. "Better get back where you belong, girl," he called to her. "Go on. Get."

The mare swished her high-set tail but otherwise did not move. Alec touched the stallion with his heels and turned him to the edge of road so they could step around her and get on with their business. The stallion resisted a moment but answered Alec's signals, perhaps as suspicious of the mare as Alec was. She waited for them to pass. Pretending to sulk, her head hanging low, she began following a few lengths behind them, almost like a lonely dog. In the field across the stream, the other two mares watched silently.

"Go home," Alec called to the mare on their tail. She raised her head, her soulful eyes fixed on the Black.

Alec kept his horse pointed ahead. "Come on, fella," he said. "We are in enough trouble already. We don't have time for this."

Alec pushed the Black into a trot, but still the mare followed. She began to canter and moved up alongside them, pushing her head close to the Black. "Hey," Alec shouted at her. "Back! Get back!"

The mare pressed closer, almost touching the Black's neck with her soft gray muzzle, then nipping the air next to him playfully. Alec kicked out his right foot to push her away. The mare swung her head and deftly avoided Alec's foot. Then with a flash of teeth, she lunged.

Alec threw out his foot once more, and this time the mare caught hold of it with her mouth. He felt her teeth through the shoe leather and jerked his foot back, losing his shoe. The mare shook her head and dashed up the road ahead, triumphantly gripping Alec's old running shoe in her mouth.

"Hey," Alec cried. "Give me that back!" He couldn't believe the mare's behavior. She was acting more like mischievous dog that had just snatched a bone from the kitchen table than a horse. It was all very peculiar, Alec thought, but more importantly the mare had his shoe, and he needed it. He wasn't about to walk out of this place barefoot. Alec put the Black into a gallop and chased after her.

"Give me that back, you nut," Alec cried.

The mare bounced up the road in front of them. It didn't appear that she was really trying to escape; it was more as if she was simply teasing and wanting them to chase her. The Black carried Alec close enough so he could lean down, reach over and get a hand on a part of the shoe that was sticking out of her mouth. The mare tugged back playfully as he yanked on the shoe, trying to free it from her clenched teeth. Finally she let go.

Alec pulled the stallion to a stop and couldn't help but laugh at the absurdity of it all. The Black snorted and drummed his hooves in the dirt. The mare squealed triumphantly and then dashed away. She veered off the road and across the open field to return to where her sisters were waiting by the side of the stream. A moment later, all three vanished into the trees bordering the far side of the pasture.

Alec jumped off the Black, mashed his shoe back into shape and then put it on again. He gave the horse a pat on the neck. "Shoe-stealing mares," Alec said. "You don't want to get mixed up with them."

He took a step back and remounted. Pointing the Black up the road, he touched the stallion with his heels and they were off. The road twisted around a sharp bend, and a short distance away Alec could see several small cottages among stands of tall trees.

Larger, gable-roofed houses were clustered around a central courtyard farther on. Alec heard a baying sound and saw sheep pastured in a field to one side of the settlement. Animals at last, he thought. What a relief. It was the first time he'd seen any animals, aside from horses, since he'd been here.

They passed through an open, unmanned gate. Outside one of the cottages, a young woman was raking leaves in the yard. As she stared at the passing stranger, Alec noticed something odd about her. Somehow her pale, pinkish skin seemed to be pulled too tight over her face, like a person who'd had bad plastic surgery. She stepped back as Alec passed, retreating all the way to the shadow of her doorway.

Alec looked around for more signs of life. Two ordinary-looking draft horses were yoked to a wooden wagon loaded with straw in a field beside the road. It was odd he hadn't seen any machines, not even a bicycle, since he'd been here, Alec thought. It really did seem as if he'd stepped back in time a couple hundred years.

They came to a village square. At the center was a marble fountain and statuary in a small garden. If this was Tarta, Alec thought, the village didn't look to be nearly as fancy a place as the city of Acracia. This neighborhood appeared a bit run-down; the gardens were smaller and not so carefully tended, and the

statuary was less elaborate and buildings less impos-
ing. A flock of geese and a herd of pigs roamed loose
around a small amphitheater.

Alec slid off the Black's back, and the stallion immediately turned his attention to munching on the garden grass. A half dozen villagers who had gathered
on a nearby porch now cautiously made their way
toward Alec, plainly wary of the visitor and his black
stallion. As in the city below, the men and women here
were all attired in sleeveless gowns with cloaks draped
over the shoulder. They appeared to be about the same
age, perhaps in their early thirties, and all slightly older
than the dwellers in the acropolis. One of them raised
his hand in a salute, then stepped forward and bowed
almost to the ground. Alec wasn't sure what to do, so
he bowed in response.

He was a big guy, with bulked-up muscles and
long, flowing blond hair; yet his eyes were old-looking,
his face crinkled with age around the edges. "English?"
the man said.

"American," Alec said. "Speak English?"

The man smiled but shook his head no. He bowed
again, then called out in the direction of the cottages
on the other side of the square. After a minute, Alec
saw Xeena hurrying his way. Karst was with her.

"Alec," she called, beckoning to him.

"Xeena! Karst!" he answered. "There you are."

Alec shook Karst's hand. Xeena's dad smiled but did not speak. He was looking at the Black as if he'd never seen the stallion before. Xeena took Alec by the arm, then turned and pulled him back in the direction of the cottages. "We need to talk," she said softly.

11

Popi

Xeena cast a look over her shoulder. She smiled and waved to the group who had met Alec and the Black inside the village square. Then she turned to Alec and lowered her voice. "Just keep walking," she said mysteriously. "I'll explain in a minute."

"How did you find us, Karst?" Alec asked. Alec waited for his friend to answer, but Karst only kept marching forward. Xeena's dad still barely seemed to recognize Alec or the Black. He kept his eyes on the stallion, his gaze wide with wonder. Alec asked again, and when Karst finally spoke, the tone of his voice sounded odd, nothing like the man Alec remembered.

"This is my home," Karst said, his English almost without accent and completely unlike Karst's normal voice. Then he bowed his head in that way everyone seemed to do around here and that usually translated into "that's all I have to say."

They came to a white cottage surrounded by big,

old trees and a lawn and garden run to seed. Xeena waved them through the open front door. Karst paused and turned to face Alec and the Black. "My home is humble but clean. Please do me the honor of allowing me to pay my respects." He showed them to a corner bedroom, and Alec held the Black steady as Karst pushed the narrow bed against the wall. Xeena covered the floor with straw. A minute later the bedroom had been transformed into a makeshift stall for the Black.

Inside the cottage, as everywhere in Acracia, the dominating theme was horses. Everything in sight was decorated with them—horse heads, rearing horses, running horses. Renderings of horses were embroidered on the pillows, carved on the posts of the banisters leading to the attic and adorned either end of the mantelpiece.

Xeena brought in a towel for Alec to dry off with and a blanket for the Black. Then she spread out a bucket of oats over a table for the stallion to eat. The Black sniffed the oats a moment and then set upon his feed.

"Welcome to my home," Karst said, his English perfect with barely a trace of accent. "All Acracia has been expecting you." Again the voice sounded unfamiliar to Alec and not at all like Karst. Could this be the same man he'd known on the film set, the one who always seemed jovial and ready for a laugh?

"Expecting me?" Alec said in exasperation. "Karst. Wake up. What's wrong with you? It's me. Alec. Xeena must have told you what happened to us."

"Yes, she told me. You are both lucky to be alive."

Alec glanced around him. "Who lives in this house? What are you doing here?"

"I told you," Karst said. "This is my home."

"Your home?" Alec said. "I don't understand."

Karst smiled again.

"You better sit down," Xeena said, pointing Alec to a chair.

Alec took a seat, and Xeena explained what had happened since he left her in the megaron. Her words came quickly as she told him how she had been on the balcony when she thought she saw her father passing by in a wagon. She'd followed him up here and then—

Alec held up his hand. "Wait a minute, Xeena. What do you mean thought you saw . . . Isn't this your dad?"

Xeena blinked and shook her head. "This is my grandfather, Popi."

Alec gazed at the man sitting in the chair opposite him, someone who could not have been much more than thirty-five years old.

"At first I thought he was my dad too," Xeena said, "just as you did. I don't understand it myself.

Popi has been trying to explain it to me ever since I got here. Popi, you tell him."

"My name is Nicholas Balastritis," the man said. "Karst Balastritis is my son. This is my granddaughter."

Alec glanced at Xeena. "It's true, Alec," she said. "He knows things that only Popi could know."

"It is going to be difficult for you to believe this," the man said, "but you must try."

"You can't be Xeena's grandfather," Alec said. "What are you, thirty-five? Thirty-six?"

"I am seventy-two years old," the man said without blinking an eye.

"I tell you it's true," Xeena said. "This is Popi. I asked him about some things that happened when I was little, and he knew all about them."

Alec held up his hand. "Please, Xeena," he said patiently. "Lots of professional fortune-tellers and phony psychics can do that, and usually it is part of some sort of scam. This place looks like a big-budget health club selling salvation and magic cures to vulnerable people. Someone is making money out of all this, believe me."

"This is no health club," the man who called himself Nicholas Balastritis said. "Acracia is a Garden of Eden. The waters here are truly blessed. Drink deeply."

"Let's talk about the money for a minute," Alec

said. "Are you saying everything is free here? How do you people pay for it all?"

Nicholas smiled, as if amused by Alec's skepticism. "Upon arriving in Acracia," he said, "people deposit their money in the bank and are given credit in the city's shops and eating places. Guests are welcome as long as they obey our laws. Strangers and trespassers are not. Once here, most guests stay for the remainder of their lives."

"Do you mean that no one ever leaves this place?" he said.

"It would be impossible to leave Acracia for most of us. And why would we even want to leave? You can keep your modern civilization, its ravages of time and old age, its wars, famine and disease. Here in the Realm, life is good. We citizens of Acracia accept that this is the best of all possible worlds. You will know this to be true if you stay with us."

"Thanks but no thanks," Alec said.

With a bow, Nicholas spoke again, his voice more humble now. "Of course, you are not an ordinary guest and may do as you wish here, but please do not dishonor my house by leaving before you can truly be made welcome." He gestured to a small empty field outside an open window. "Look, please," he said. "Allow your horse to graze a few minutes before you go. The grass is rich and green here in Tarta."

Alec welcomed the chance to get outside and try to digest all he had just heard. He led the Black to the pasture and realized that it was later than he thought; the sun was already descending behind the mountains. Once again, ominous-looking rain clouds were gathering in the sky to the north and a not-so-distant rumbling filled the sky. A minute later, it started to rain.

Alec brought the Black inside, toweled him off and rubbed him out again. Nicholas watched Alec as he worked. "He is a fantastic animal, your Bucephalus," Nicholas said. "One truly worthy of Alexander and the messenger of the gods of Greece."

"I am from America, not Greece," Alec said.

Nicholas smiled. "No matter. The fact is you are in Acracia now. Your coming was foretold by the Oracle, and you are here."

"We got caught in a river, were swept through the mountain and almost drowned. That is the only reason we are here," Alec said.

"That is also a sign that was foretold."

Alec looked at Xeena. From her mesmerized expression, it appeared that she really did think this man was her grandfather and that the wild things he was saying could be true.

"Okay," Alec said, "believe what you want. You are right. I am a messenger from the gods. My message is that you guys are great. Thanks for everything.

Keep up the good work. Now how the heck do we get out of this place?"

"Please, Alec," Nicholas said. "Do not be so quick to judge us. There is much to learn here." His words were punctuated by another long rumble outside.

More thunder, Alec thought, though he was surprised that it shook the furniture and rattled the dishes.

The Black whinnied. "Easy boy," Alec said. The stallion bobbed his head and leaned into Alec's shoulder. "That's it. Just some thunder. Easy now."

The sounds of wind and rain grew stronger. Not much sense in trying to make a run for it now, Alec thought. He watched the Black nose around in the fresh grain Xeena brought him. The stallion didn't seem anxious to go back outside just yet either.

No, Alec decided. The smart thing to do was to wait. However nutty this place seemed, he couldn't see harm in anything they were doing. Alec trusted the Black's instincts far above his own, and the stallion didn't seem to be too alarmed about being here.

Later that evening at dinner, they ate corn and potato soup, grapes, cheese and yogurt, everything fresh and flavorful. As they ate, Xeena told Nicholas about their jobs on the *Young Alexander* film set and about meeting Alec and the Black. She explained that the

Black was a famous racehorse and that only Alec could ride him.

"Like Bucephalus and Alexander," Nicholas said. "Again I say this is no mere coincidence. It is your destiny to have found your way here."

Alec started to say something and then held back. Better to go along, he thought, at least until he could find a way out of here. It wasn't up to him to prove Nicholas was a fraud, and who knew? Maybe he wasn't.

Alec looked down into his glass and swirled the contents. The water tasted so clean and pure it was almost sweet. Certainly it contained minerals of some kind. Alec figured he'd been drinking it since yesterday with no ill effects, so there didn't seem to be any reason to stop now. Quite the opposite, he thought. In some ways he couldn't remember when he'd felt as strong and clearheaded. There was no disputing that he had almost forgotten about the twisted ankle that had troubled him so much yesterday.

Nicholas raised his glass. "Blessed by the milk of the sacred mares, the waters of Acracia will cure sickness and will restore youth and health. It seems an inexcusable loss that the secret of the water is not shared with mankind. Science could tell us much if studies could be made—if only we could get the message out."

"Why don't you?" Alec said.

"It's not that simple," Nicholas said with a wry smile. Despite his youthful appearance, his face was that of someone who had seen that life is a much greater riddle than most people suspect.

"Perhaps you are the one Fate has chosen to do just that, the courier who will take our message to the outside world," Nicholas said. "Perhaps that is what the Oracle meant about a messenger. Perhaps Acracia is sending the message, and not receiving it."

Night had fallen and the rain continued. Alec cleared the dishes and Nicholas made coffee while Xeena set up a backgammon board. Alec sipped a cup of thick, sweet coffee and went into the Black's room and looked out the window. He could hear water dripping and leaves rattling and could see dark branches swaying in the wind as it rose and fell.

As he gazed at the world outside, his supper settled in his stomach and mellowed his mood. What a fascinating place this is, he thought. The Black seemed to be enjoying it too. Maybe Nicholas wasn't so off base, after all. Maybe he should spend a little more time here and try to find out what this place was all about.

Lightning flashed across the sky and more thunder rumbled. The sounds snapped Alec back to reality. What were these thoughts in his head?

Stay here, in this place? What was he thinking? He didn't belong here. The people in Acracia weren't just guests in a resort. They were part of some bizarre health cult. Even more alarming was the realization that something inside him was on the verge of succumbing to the idea of staying here. It was almost as if some unknown force was trying to rub away all his concerns and responsibilities. His thoughts about the past were jumbled and confused, though he felt incredibly alert in the present. Deep in the back of his mind, a voice told him this wasn't right, that he wasn't thinking correctly, that these weren't his thoughts inside his head but someone else's.

He went to the basin to splash some water on his face, water clear as winter ice in the candlelight. Whatever was happening to his body, it was his imagination that now needed soothing more than anything.

He returned to the living room where Xeena and Nicholas continued their board game on a low table by the fire. It was a lovely domestic scene—a cozy room lit by the soft glow of firelight, everything warm and safe and dry. Even the Black seemed relaxed. Alec fought to keep his mind alert and his guard up.

As the night wore on, Xeena and Nicholas talked together over their game, easily switching back and forth between English and Greek. Soon Alec found he was getting sleepy. Nicholas offered up his bed, but

Alec said he wanted to stick close to the Black. Nicholas said he understood and brought blankets to keep Alec warm. Xeena found a place on the couch in front of the fire.

Alec lay beside the quietly dozing stallion. He resolved to be up before dawn so they could start the journey away from here, rain or no rain. Pulling his covers up to his chin, Alec listened to the raindrops falling outside like plucked violin strings. Soon he was drifting off, again returning in his dreams to the banquet in the megaron. He could see the swirling figures of dancing horses and people, the slender form and veiled face of the priestess Cyrene as she ran her hands over the albino mare. Then they were soaring up over the gardens together, circling higher and higher, past the guard tower, past the acropolis wall. Around them flower blossoms blew through the air like dry leaves caught in an updraft. . . .

Alec was awakened by an explosion of sound, first the fierce cry of the Black and then another sound even more forceful.

At first Alec thought it must be thunder, until he realized he had been thrown out of bed and was now lying on the floor. No mere thunderstorm could do that. There were crashing noises coming from the other side of the house and sounds of breaking glass.

The floor beneath him was rising and falling as if washed by rippling waves. Hunks of plaster were breaking loose from the walls and ceiling. It wasn't the first time Alec had experienced something like this, and instantly he guessed what was happening.

Earthquake!

He looked around the room. The door was off its hinges, and there was no sign of the Black.

Alec screamed for his horse. The ground was so unsteady beneath him that he didn't even try to move. All he could do was hang on to the floor and wait for the tremor to pass. Again Alec heard the wild clarion call of the stallion from out in the night, only this time another horse shrilled a reply.

Finally the floor ceased shaking enough that Alec could move. He leaped to his feet and raced outside over the still-unsteady ground. The rain had ceased, and a bright, full moon illuminated the shapes of two rearing horses. One was the Black. The other was the ghostly albino mare Celera. They seemed to be dancing in the air, several feet above the rolling moonlit earth below. Then they turned and dashed away across the field.

12

Nocturne

The Black tore into the night. He was free again, and the ground had ceased to shake beneath his hooves. His nostrils filled with the unearthly scent of the mare running before him. She sped toward a high wooden fence spanning the far end of the pasture, glimmers of moonlight splashing her pale white coat.

The mare barely slowed as she gathered herself for the jump. Then she sprang into the air and was flying over the top rail to come down lightly on the other side. Instantly she was off again in full stride, galloping along the road out of Tarta. The Black burst into a run and charged the fence behind her. He leaped forward, taking the fence at a gallop. Touching down, he skipped into the air again, stretching out his neck, his great strides swallowing up the dark ground beneath him.

There was a sharp curve in the road ahead, and the mare followed it. The Black rounded the bend less than a dozen lengths behind her. Straightening out

NOCTURNE 173

again, he extended his stride and continued on at full speed.

The Black threw back his head and gave a piercing cry, calling in vain to the ghostly apparition running before him. As he closed in to overtake the defiant mare, the albino suddenly broke off the road, vanishing where a trail led into the woods. The Black ducked under a branch to follow until his way was slowed and finally blocked by snakelike vines hanging from the branches overhead. All at once, he could barely move. The vines caught his neck and pulled at his legs. Thorns stung his flesh. He fought to break free, finally escaping the tangle of vines and bolting up the trail.

The path led to a moonlit clearing. Breaking into the open, he began sniffing the air, seeking some scent to tell him where to go. Not finding it, he cried out in frustration and burst into a run, dashing off in one direction, then another. He pulled up finally and waited. Soon his ears caught faint, tinkling sounds in the wind. There was an odor there as well, something unknown but somehow familiar and inviting.

Following the strange signs in the breeze, the stallion could soon make out the dark shapes of horses moving in a glade at the far end of the clearing, a pair of mares dancing in the moonlight. They passed each other with even strides. Their tails flicked back and forth, whisking to a soft rhythm pulsing in the air.

The cloaked figure of a young woman stood on a large rock near them. She held a horseshoe-shaped object close to her chest. From it emanated the soft raindrop-like sounds that had led him there. The Black watched and waited as the mares moved in time and revolved around each other. Though the albino wasn't there, he sensed she wasn't far off.

For many moments, all was still but for the padding of hooves in the grass, the relaxed breathing of the horses and the soft strains of music floating on the air. The mares were aware of the stallion, but they did not stop their dancing or break their formation. Then one turned to him. She pranced in place and bobbed her head as if inviting him to join them. The other mare continued her soft parading and watched him with sly, secretive glances.

There was a sudden drumming of hooves. The melodic strains of the strings stopped. A cry cut the air and standing beside the cloaked woman's perch was the albino. Her cry and sudden appearance unsettled the intricate passage of the two mares, and they suddenly collided into each other.

The Black replied and stepped into the center of the glade as the mares retreated. He sensed more than saw the albino who stared at him from the far end of the glade. An aura completely unknown to him surrounded her, and the Black stood spellbound, his gaze

fixed upon her. She switched her tail, but that was the
only part of her that seemed to be alive. Her legs and
even her mane were as still as lifeless stone. She stood
silent, not even seeming to breathe.

The stallion gazed at the vision before him. Her
ruby eyes were open, yet they were not focused on anything. It was an unseeing gaze, as if turned inward. The
other mares clustered to one side, nickering to each
other and content to stand by and watch the confrontation between the two silent, motionless figures
locked in their moonlit reveries.

Finally the albino broke from her pose and noticed him. The stallion caught the look and cried out.
The mare replied with a fierce neigh of her own, a
high, defiant cry let loose upon the night. It was not
a call for solace or a cry for understanding, but a claim
of dominion.

Rising up on her hind legs, the albino pawed the
air, as if trying to claw her way up into the starry sky,
into the lonesome depths of night. When at last she
came down again, she glared at the stallion. Her eyes
seemed to burn like red-hot coals. Then she was off
and running over the moon-splashed grass. With a
playful whinny, she taunted the stallion to follow.

The Black raced after her, but cautiously. Somehow he felt as if he had been here before, as if he had
returned to some long-lost place that now welcomed

him home after a long, weary journey. All was quiet in his ears. Even his hoofbeats sounded muffled and distant to him now. Ahead of him, the mare seemed to float over the dark ground as she dashed away.

With blowing breath, the stallion accelerated after her, and the speed broke the spell that had been holding him back. All at once, his nostrils caught new smells in the air, scents that spoke of others, and of danger, but he did not stop or slow his headlong charge. All his senses were focused ahead as he closed to within a length of the mare. Just as he was about to overtake her, the pair of horses reached the end of the field.

The mare swung hard to the right. Suddenly they were sprinting along a line of fence and toward a narrow passageway opening into the adjacent pasture. The mare squeezed through the gap in the high fence. The Black followed a step behind.

The two horses burst into the pasture. Immediately they were running neck and neck toward a cluster of moonlit shadows in the center of the field. It was a herd of grazing horses, mares and their foals. The startled herd burst into motion, sprinting for a dark line of trees looming in the distance. Leading them was the young gray stallion who had challenged the Black the day before. The herd raced ahead in a mad frenzy. The smells from their steaming bodies told the Black they were running out of blind panic.

The Black and the albino rushed ahead to join the others, and in an instant the herd was racing as one. The horses' fear pushed them to frightening speeds. An overpowering instinct drove the stallion's headlong rush to lead them. Heaving bodies rolled beside him, plunging forward, matching him stride for stride.

The pasture narrowed. Suddenly there was a loud clamor, and a new smell fueled the air—fire, the element the two-legged beasts held so sacred. There was a burst of light, and in front of the herd stood a line of men. They were standing shoulder to shoulder, shouting and waving torches and long, pointed sticks. The horses careened to a jumbled stop.

The appearance of the men made the mares scatter. Before the Black could join them in their flight, the young gray stallion wheeled and struck out at him. The Black turned to face his attacker. He rose on his hind legs, and the gray reared to meet him. Their heavy bodies collided with a terrible impact. They hung together in the air a moment and then crashed to the ground.

The Black was moving forward to renew the fight when the pack of men came toward him. Distracted by his arrogant pursuit of the mare and the attack of the gray, the Black was caught by surprise. The stallion reared as the men formed a circle around him. He had known their kind before, two-legged creatures who would rather fight than run. A long, snakelike rope flew through the air suddenly. It opened its mouth and coiled around his neck. Another flying snake hissed overhead and wrapped around him.

Soon the rest of the herd was gone, and the Black was left fighting the snake ropes and the men who held him. The stallion boldly threw off one of the ropes, but another caught his hind leg. More men came to join the others. The Black could see the albino running off behind the men. She paused to look back. Lifting her proud head, she uttered a high-pitched, almost sorrowful neigh, then turned and bolted into the night.

13

Dark Visions

After watching the Black race off with Celera, Alec had run inside the cottage, pulled on his sweater and jumped into his shoes. Nicholas and Xeena followed him as he dashed back outside.

"It's that mare again," Alec said. "She's lured him off, just like she did at the river."

"We'll help you find him," Nicholas said. "Wait a moment for me to get some shoes on and—"

"I can't wait," Alec said. He looked at the broken door and a deep crack that had formed in the wall. "What happened? Was that really an earthquake?"

"I am afraid so," Nicholas said. "We have had tremors before but never anything like this."

Without another word, Alec turned and ran out into the night to search for his horse. A stiff wind was blowing away the last few clouds, and a full moon brightened the landscape. To one side he could see the tower of Tarta was still standing, but he could also hear the distant sounds of voices shouting. Smoke was swirling up into the sky, and there was the glow of light as if a building had caught fire.

Alec turned away from the town and jogged off into the night, quickly picking up the trail of the two horses. He followed the tracks to the road leading down to Acracia.

Everywhere along the road were signs of devastation from the earthquake that had shaken the mountain. Fences were down and stray sheep and goats gathered in the road bleating. A giant cedar tree had been lifted out of the ground and lay toppled on its side. A barrier wall next to the road had collapsed. Alec ran along, trying to stay focused, following the trail the stallion and the mare had left in the wet dirt.

All at once, Alec heard the drumming of hooves behind him. He turned, thinking it was the Black, but it was not the stallion or Celera. Charging down upon him was the shoe-stealing mare he and the Black had met on the road earlier that day.

Alec held up his hands. "Whoa," he called to her. The mare splashed to a stop in a mud puddle only a few feet away. As before, she wore no tack whatsoever, not even a halter. The mare beat her forehooves on the wet ground.

"What are you doing here?" Alec said.

The mare bounced back and forth on her hooves, then side to side.

"Sorry, girl," Alec said. "I don't want to dance right now, and your boyfriend already took off."

The mare lowered her head and came to Alec. She stopped jigging and stood still before him, as if inviting him to mount up and go for a ride. Alec didn't need to think about it long. If he was going to catch up with the Black and Celera, he would do better on horseback than on foot. Alec trusted he could handle this unfamiliar horse as he had so many others, green ones to mean ones, at the farm and on the track.

Alec spoke to the mare, then touched her and leaned his forearms on her warm, wet back. Her coat felt coarse, almost like rough fur. She did not move away from him.

"Okay, Shoe Thief," he said. "You behave now. That's it. You're a good girl." The mare looked over her shoulder at him, listening to his soft words as if she'd heard them a thousand times before. Then she straightened her neck and waited for him to make his move.

In one swift step, Alec pivoted his body and vaulted onto the mare's short back. The instant his legs wrapped around her, she was off and running, not in the direction the Black and Celera's trail was leading but in the opposite direction, back toward Tarta. Using soft pressure from his legs, hands and voice, Alec finally managed to get her slowed down and turned in the right direction.

Soon they were splashing ahead through the puddles and loping along the road back to the citadel. The mare moved willingly, but Alec was not fool enough to believe he had much control over her. Even the best riders could be unseated while riding bareback, even on a horse they knew well. And this horse was unlike any Alec had ever ridden. He gripped the white mane and pressed himself closer to her neck. There was a strange, heavy smell about her, a wet muskiness more akin to some wild forest animal than a horse. He tried to stay in rhythm with her shuffling strides. At least he was covering some ground, he thought. He shifted his weight in response to the mare's action, trying to keep his body centered and his legs ready to answer any sudden change in direction or speed. The wet mane whipped back into his face as the mare broke into a gallop. She was not fighting him, but there was something more than untamed about this petulant mare who had stolen his shoe earlier that day. Had she ever carried a rider before? Alec wondered. Through his legs and seat, he could feel shudders of pleasure running through her like intermittent waves of electricity. To Alec it was almost like a purring sensation, as if he were seated atop a contented mountain lion rather than a mare. The shoe thief glided smoothly along, barely seeming to notice the human clinging to her back like a giant bug.

Alec had no idea where she was taking him but could only hope that her instincts led her to the other horses and that the Black was with them. Her ears were angled back, and she bounded ahead, not like a flight animal but with all the intense focus and grace of a predator on the hunt.

The muddy ground passed beneath him in a blur as the mare carried Alec past the sacred pastures to a place where the road forked, one fork descending to the acropolis, the other leading farther up the mountain. Alec wondered if the Black and Celera had come this way.

The mare barely slowed as she swung her body hard to follow the fork climbing up the mountain. She careened forward along the moonlit road, running fast and close to being out of control.

A cloud covered the moon, and too late Alec saw what looked like a dark wall ahead. It was a fallen tree stretching from one side of the road to the other. Alec could tell the mare wasn't going to stop, and he had no time to prepare for the jump. The mare took off without hesitating, soaring into the air, her legs brushing through the tops of the branches. She staggered only slightly as she touched down, but it was enough to bounce Alec forward and unseat him from her slick back. Jarred loose from his mount, Alec was launched into the air. He just managed to pull his legs up under him before he slammed into the ground, rolled and came to a stop.

Alec lay motionless for a minute, gasping for breath as the mare continued flying up the road. He crawled to his feet and for a moment could not even remember who he was or how he came to be here. Then the buzzing between his ears slowly subsided, and he recalled the wild ride on the mare and his search for the Black. He tried to keep his mind focused, but his thoughts remained as scattered as windblown leaves.

Alec stared into the night, trying to get hold of himself. He'd had the wind knocked out of him and was scraped up and covered with mud, but otherwise he was unhurt. He took a cautious step forward, testing each leg before putting weight on it. Satisfied that everything seemed to be in working order, he immediately began searching the road for tracks. After a minute, he found one set of hoofprints, then another, then a third. One set Alec felt fairly certain were those of his horse. In spite of the moonlight painting the muddy road, it was still too dark to be positive.

Alec continued on, not sure of where he was

going. At least there were still tracks on the road, Alec thought. If the trail had broken off into the woods, it would have been almost impossible to follow. He hurried along the route up the mountain, again asking himself how in the world he ever ended up here.

The road wound through the forest, and soon he came to a long row of neat, orderly houses that seemed to be leaning into each other for support. The dwellings were made of white stone and built in low two- and three-story stacks against the base of a cliff wall, like small apartments. The arched shadows of their doorways stood out against the white walls in the pools of bright moonlight. Not a single light shown in any of the windows. There were none of the ornate fountains or plazas here as in the city below, or even the lush but overgrown gardens of Tarta. Here all was simplicity itself, white and clean-looking but humble. Smoke rolled out the chimneys, and there was a smell in the air Alec could not identify. All was still except for the sound of his own footsteps. Just keep moving, he told himself.

The trail of fresh hoofprints led straight down the center of the village. Alec saw no signs of collapsed walls or buildings here, or anything that even looked damaged. Perhaps the earth tremors had not reached this high up.

At the other end of the main street was an old

man shrouded in a blanket and sitting on the ground, his back propped up against a wall. The man looked very skinny, little more than a skeleton in ragged clothes. He was the first person who appeared much over thirty years old that Alec had seen since he came here. Alec spoke to the man, but the old guy seemed to be asleep.

Alec passed the last house on the far side of the strange little town and looked toward the summit of Mt. Atnos, home to the Oracle and the temple of Diomedes. He could see little dots of light moving around the faint outline of the temple. What were they? Alec wondered. People carrying flashlights? Perhaps a rescue party of some sort? Was that too much to hope for?

The street became a wide path that led farther up the mountain. There were more rocks than trees here. In the pale moonlight splashed over the ground, he could see telltale traces of horses—fresh manure and muddy hoofprints along the path.

Alec heard something that made him stop, the distant cry of a horse coming from somewhere among the lofty peaks. Could it have been the Black? He waited in vain for some clue telling him where to go, straining his ears in the dark, his heart pounding in his chest. Gazing up to the temple, again he felt as if he had stepped back in time and was now locked on some predetermined path, one he had no choice but to follow, one leading unstoppably upward to the summit of Mt. Atnos and the temple of the ancient horse master Diomedes.

The passage to the top zigzagged higher, and Alec saw more lights. People were carrying torches, he realized, though it was difficult to make out much more than that. The lights were clustering around a dark shape, what Alec at first thought might be a small windmill built in a cleared area along the slope of the mountain. Or perhaps it was a very large statue of some sort. Despite the bright moonlight, it was impossible for Alec to tell exactly what the object could be.

All at once, the torches were tossed onto the structure. Even from a quarter mile away, Alec could hear a whooshing sound as the windmill burst into flame. A moment later he smelled burning oil in the wind.

The fire spread rapidly, running along the edges. It was only after the object was completely consumed by fire that Alec could finally see what it was—an enormous wooden horse that now burned like a beacon in the night.

Built into the mountaintop above the flaming horse figure were columns that rose to a domed roof, the temple of Diomedes. Alec couldn't see what was inside, but he could hear a chorus of voices singing somewhere not far off in the dark.

Alec crept closer. The moon was very bright, and now the burning horse also added light to the nocturnal landscape. He kept to the shadows, unsure of what he should do next. He could see movement on the lawn in front of the temple, people dressed in robes, and there were horses, too, all riderless. It must be some sort of ceremony, he thought. Perhaps the burning of the wooden horse was an offering of some sort, or perhaps it was meant to invoke the legendary Trojan horse.

The droning murmur of chanting drifted in the air and was soon joined by the soft beat of drums. Alec could make out figures circling the towering effigy, swaying and waving their long arms across the glow of the fire.

Then, above the noises of the ritual, Alec heard a sharp, piercing sound ring through the air, the war cry of an enraged stallion. It was the Black—he was sure of that now—and he was close by.

Alec followed the sound. The Black was surrounded by a crowd of Acracian guards bearing spears and torches. The men had managed to get ropes around the Black's neck and one hind leg and were trying to force him into submission. They swarmed around like insects as they tried to overpower the enraged stallion. The Black twisted his body. Rearing up, he fought the ropes that held him and screamed again.

Alec picked up a stick from the ground for a weapon and charged headlong at the men in a desperate attempt to free his horse. He ran into the crowd, swinging the stick like a club and crying out at the top of his lungs.

Alec slammed into one man and clubbed at the hands of another. The Black shook one of the ropes loose and reared again, his coat gleaming like black satin in the firelight. Throwing all his body weight back onto his forelegs, he brought his hooves to the ground with an explosive crash. The men scattered and the stallion broke free. A moment later he was running off into the night. Two of the men chased after the stallion, and the others turned their attention to Alec.

14

The Temple of Diomedes

Suddenly a voice from beyond the group barked an order and the guards backed off. It was Spiro. He shouted a reprimand at the men and dismissed them with a wave of his hand.

"Dear, dear," the governor's chamberlain said, his voice softening as he addressed Alec. "I am terribly sorry, Herr Alex. Please forgive those overeager fools. They were only acting under orders."

Alec had a hard time keeping his anger in check. "Fools?" he said. "Those men are dangerous. This *place* is dangerous. This is the second time my horse has been attacked."

"Medio is very protective of this area. The temple of Diomedes is the heart of Acracia. None may come here unless they are granted special permission by the governor himself."

"I didn't want to come here in the first place, and neither did my horse," Alec said. "We are just looking for a way out of here. If those security guards of yours hadn't interfered, we'd be long gone already. Now the Black has taken off again and—"

"Yes," Spiro said. "I would imagine that neither the bonds of human love nor Acracian walls could hold the likes of him for long. But Fire-eyes is here. Perhaps your Bucephalus is with her. At any rate, he cannot be far off."

Spiro gestured to the temple and beamed at Alec with polite courtesy. "It is good to see you here, and I am glad you could join us, oh messenger of the gods."

Alec shook his head. Here we go again, he thought. "No, I'd rather not . . ."

Spiro smiled and took Alec by the arm. "Now that you are here at the temple, I really must insist," he said.

Alec shrugged off the man's hand, losing his patience. "No," he said. "Now *I* must insist. Who are you anyway? How do I get out of this place?"

Spiro stepped back and bowed his head apologetically. "You came by way of the white road and must leave by way of the red road, through the gateway at the temple of Mt. Atnos. Thus spoke the Oracle."

"There is a road to the other side of the mountain?" Alec said. "That's terrific. Red road. White road. I don't care if it's the pink road with purple polka dots on it, as long as it gets me out of here."

"That's the way out for you," Spiro said, "the best and only true way. But I was hoping you would change your mind and stay with us a time. If you really must go, be assured we will await your return."

"Fine," Alec said. "We will all get together next year and have a big reunion. Right now I need to get back to work, and I am not leaving without Xeena and my horse."

Spiro nodded. "Of course," he said.

"So where is this road?" Alec said. "How do we reach it? Is it this way?"

"This way," Spiro said, leading Alec onto the temple grounds.

Spiro gestured up to the moonlit temple as they walked along. "I beg you to take stock of this place while you can, messenger," he said. "The ancient world has been reborn here. Not retold as in a play or mocked in a show, or even imitated in some meaningless ceremony, but born again in the flesh, as you will be. Wait and see, young Alexander, your destiny will be fulfilled again."

Alec's frustrations boiled over. "You people are crazy," he said. "Please listen to me, Spiro. One last time, I am not a messenger and my name is not Alex. It is Alec. Alec Ramsay. I am a jockey. I was born in New York. My horse's name is the Black, not Bucephalus."

Spiro looked at Alec. His face hardened, and it

appeared that Alec's words were finally sinking in. He shook his head with disappointment. "Do you mean to say you still believe your coming here was just an accident, that it wasn't preordained somehow?"

"Preordained by whom, the gods? I just can't buy that."

"Then the time has come for you to leave," Spiro said.

"That's fine with me," Alec said. "I appreciate your hospitality but—"

"Of course, Alec," Spiro said, bowing his head, then gesturing to the fire on the mountain summit. "This way, please."

Alec knew he wasn't arguing with a lunatic. The man's intelligence was perfectly clear, and Alec knew he was sincere and believed what he was saying, as mad as it might sound.

Spiro led the way ahead and spoke to Alec as they walked along. "Of course, you may do as you wish here, messenger," he said, his voice becoming more serious. "But it is my duty to warn you. If you fail to pay homage to the gods and ask their blessings, you will never see your land, your friends or your home again. Once you have honored the gods of heaven, then and only then will they grant the passage you desire."

"And how am I supposed to pay homage to something I don't believe in?" Alec asked.

"Once you have seen the truth," Spiro said, "perhaps you will believe."

"The truth?" Alec said. "What is that supposed to mean?"

Spiro did not answer.

The ancient temple was clearly lit by the glow of the burning horse effigy. Vines climbed up the stone columns all the way to the domed roof. Even the steps leading up to the temple were covered with a tangled web of vegetation. Small crowds of Acracians grouped together at the temple base and spread out around the clearing. All wore masks, and some were crowned with goat and deer horns. Others wore simple pasteboard masks cut in the likeness of wolves and mountain lions. Many were in costume.

At the top of the steps was a small pavilion and throne where a figure sat presiding over the spectacle. By the man's size, Alec guessed it was Medio, though it was impossible to tell for certain as the person was wearing a mask, a grotesque thing made of metal with a wide-open mouth. A small, gilded sword hung at his side.

Medio rose from his throne and descended the temple steps. As he reached the bottom step, he was joined on his right by the albino mare Celera, her red eyes gleaming in the firelight. Then a cloaked figure stepped from the crowd gathered around the flaming horse. She alone was unmasked, wearing only a sheer veil over her face. It was Cyrene, the priestess who had interpreted Celera's prophecies during the banquet. She moved with small, even steps to stand at Medio's left.

At a gesture from their leader, the crowd proceeded up the stairs and into the temple. Alec joined them. Once inside, Medio raised his arms and beckoned for Alec and Spiro to approach him. "I believe King Diomedes would like to have a word with you," Spiro said.

"King Diomedes?" Alec said. "Isn't that Medio?"

"Here at the temple mount, the governor is the earthly embodiment of Diomedes," Spiro said.

"Fine," Alec said, trying to sound as brave as he could. "I'd like to speak with him too."

Spiro touched Alec on the back to gently urge him forward.

The masked monarch pronounced a greeting, and Spiro translated the message—that Alec was an honored guest and that his message would be heard.

Alec looked at Spiro. "Tell him thanks," he said. "This is a great place he has here, but I really must be off. Tell him I have business to tend to elsewhere, other messages to deliver, a family back home."

Spiro translated as a chant went up from the crowd, words Alec did not understand. Then the masked monarch spoke again, his tone stern now.

"He says he understands your concerns but that you must ask for guidance from the Oracle before you go," Spiro said. "With your permission, I will ask her if it is an auspicious time for you to travel."

Upon hearing Spiro's question, Cyrene moved closer to Celera. She lowered her eyes and pressed her cheek against the mare's ivory neck. She uttered some words, and Spiro turned to Alec. "The Oracle says the time has not yet come for you to leave us."

Alec took a deep breath, mindful of the power in the ritual that was going on around him. Yes, he believed if there was magic anywhere, it was here, and something inside him ached to go with it, to let go, to join in and be part of it. The sensation thrilled as much as frightened him. Celera held him in her gaze, her head tilted slightly, her ruby eyes glowing orange in the moonlight, a vision of imperious equine beauty. From deep within him, Alec found the courage to speak up.

"What does she want?" Alec asked.

"Do you mean what does she want of you?" Spiro said.

"No," Alec said. "I mean what does *she* want, the Oracle."

Spiro looked at Alec with surprise. "The Oracle? The Oracle does not want. She only sees the future."

"I don't care to know the future," Alec said. "I am only asking what she wants, she herself. Could you ask her that for me, please?"

Spiro reluctantly translated Alec's words, and the priestess read the mare's soft murmurings, the tapping of hooves and flicking of ears. The priestess dropped her head, her voice quavering and soft as she interpreted the Oracle's words. When she stopped speaking, a collective gasp went up from the throng gathered there. Medio raised his arms and gave a command for quiet. Finally Spiro turned to Alec. "The Oracle says she wants to be with you," he said, "to be like you, to be as you are, to live as you live, but most of all to die as you will die."

To die as he would die, Alec thought. What did that mean?

Spiro bowed his head and backed away. The crowd pressed back and turned their masked faces to avert their eyes as the mare looked out upon them. Only Medio and Cyrene dared hold their ground in her presence now. The mare fixed her attention on Alec. Again she locked him in her fiery gaze, and at that moment he knew he was looking at an animal unlike any other. Despite her beauty, there was an aspect of deadly violence about her, a quiet threat that he never sensed in any horse before, even in the most war-like of stallions.

Medio's voice rang out in the silence to break the spell that the Oracle's words had cast over the gathering. Then the governor turned and led the way to the far end of the temple and down the stairs on the other side. Alec and the rest of the crowd followed him.

A natural basin was tucked into the mountain on this side of the temple, a large amphitheater with a hundred-yard-wide, crater-like pit in the center. Some of the masked revelers hurried to take up positions on the slope of the mountain above the steep walls of the pit. Medio, Celera, Cyrene and the rest of the governor's entourage strode ceremoniously through the amphitheater to the rim of the pit, stopping at a stone-pillared gate with a flat roof built at its edge. The gate loomed large in the moonlight, more than twelve feet wide, the carved stone covered with inscriptions and astrological signs.

Alec watched and waited, knowing he must play along and stay ready for the appropriate time to make his move. He was determined to find the Black, get back to Xeena and make their escape. But if there was another way out of this place, a road or some passageway through the mountain, he knew he must find it.

From out of the crowd behind Medio came two

people shrouded in white robes, a skinny, frail-looking old man and woman. They stepped forward and stood before the governor. They were by far the oldest people Alec had seen since he came here. Alec wasn't sure but the man could have been the same one he had seen sleeping in the streets of the village he had passed through earlier.

The couple bowed their heads as Medio spoke. Cyrene moved to stand before the couple and drew back the veil hiding her face. It was the first time Alec had really seen what the priestess looked like, as she had remained veiled throughout the banquet in the megaron. As with the mare, Alec felt almost helpless before her, unable to look away from her. A chill ran down his spine as he realized he was looking at the most beautiful woman he had ever seen, a goddess as impersonal as a force of nature. It was as if Cyrene *were* Nature herself. What was the woman's connection to Celera? he wondered. Master? Servant? Equal? Twin?

In the young woman's hands was a simple wicker basket full of flowers. The blossoms were strung together into necklaces, like Hawaiian leis. Medio reached down into the basket, took out two of the necklaces and draped one each around the necks of the old couple. They bowed again and backed away humbly.

A moment later, the old couple was escorted by a

pair of guards to the gate. The guards stood back as
the couple held hands and hobbled silently through the
stone pillars like sleepwalkers. Then they disappeared
within the dark, yawning shadows falling from the
slab of carved stone roofing the gate.

There was a noise Alec couldn't identify that was
quickly drowned out by a cheer from the crowd rim-
ming the arena. A chorus of voices broke into song.
Drums and pipes sprang to life, stirring the air with
frenzied rhythm.

Alec didn't understand. "Where did they go?" he
asked Spiro.

"See for yourself," the chamberlain said.

Alec walked to the edge of the pit and looked inside it. The drums hammered louder, joined by more
singing. Now he could see inside the gate where a path
led out to the precipice and to a steep chute made of
weathered stone. The slide ended at the floor of the pit,
which was like a bowl-shaped arena about the size of
the banquet hall of the megaron.

Something was moving over the floor of the pit. It
looked like a small herd of horses, some of the same
ones Alec had seen at the banquet in the megaron,
including Shoe Thief and her two sisters. The young
gray stallion was there as well.

What had happened to the old couple after their
big send-off by Medio and Cyrene? Had they fallen

down the slide? Where were they now? He finally noticed them in the shadows near the bottom of the slide.

The spectators raised their voices, calling out the horses' names, encouraging them on like racetrack fans at the finish of a big race. A sick feeling rose inside Alec as he suddenly realized the true nature of the drama being played out here before him.

The horses had spotted the man and woman now, and Alec watched in disbelief as they ran down the old couple. In seconds, the horses began tearing into their victims' flesh with their teeth, shaking their prey as a pack of hungry wolves or pride of lions might. It was a scene out of hell. This was the red road that Spiro had been talking about, Alec realized, the road to sacrifice and violent death. The red road was the road of blood.

After a moment, one of the mares looked up from her ghastly meal, her muzzle smeared with gore. Throwing back her head, she screamed wildly in her triumph, her savage cry ringing out into the night.

Alec reeled away from the horrific sight, but he didn't get far. Medio's authoritative voice boomed a command, and Alec was taken in hand by two strong-armed Acracian guards and ushered to where the mad governor was standing at the foot of his throne.

Alec fought against his captors, but the guards held him still and he could not break free. Medio stepped closer, close enough that Alec could smell his foul breath. In his hands was another necklace made of flowers. Medio raised the necklace ceremoniously above him and gestured to the moon. He said a few words to the gathered throng and lowered the ring of flowers over Alec's head, pressing it down onto his shoulders. Then Medio signaled to the guards, who instantly began dragging Alec toward the gate, the sacrificial pit, the road that Alec now understood led to imminent death, a horrific death unlike any he ever could have imagined. To be torn limb from limb and eaten alive . . .

Alec searched for an ally in the crowd of masked faces edging closer to the rim of the arena. The demon revelers stamped their feet. They elbowed each other out of the way, coming as close to the precipice as they dared, swaying to the music and nodding their horned heads. The scent of blood filled the air.

In a desperate effort to survive, Alec cried out and struggled against the arms forcing him forward. Outnumbered and alone, he was lifted off the ground and carried over to the ceremonial stone gate and the top of the slide leading down into the pit.

He jerked his body against the tight grips on his arms and legs, determined to fight until the end. Slipping one leg free, he brought his heel down as hard as he could on one of the men carrying him. It struck something that felt like a man's leg. The man stumbled and lost his hold. The others became unsteady. Alec wrenched an elbow free and kicked his foot again, then brought his elbow down as hard as he could on whatever was in reach. The fury of Alec's resistance startled his bearers, and they collapsed in a pile.

Alec landed on his back, but at least he was on top of the others. He rolled off, crawled back through the gate and looked for a place to run. . . .

15

The Red Road

After his escape from the man-beasts, the Black had resolved to stay hidden. He did not fear the two-legged ones or their rope snakes or pointed sticks, but he had no intention of seeking revenge for his treatment at their hands. He had found his way to this rocky peak where he could see all that passed beneath him. Here he would wait and watch. The pain in his shoulder was minor. The stick had only grazed him, and the bleeding had already ceased to flow from it.

The stallion gazed out into the starry night beyond the mountain peaks and then down at the dark world of rocks and trees below. It seemed the man-beasts had given up the chase. And if they came again, he knew he could evade them. The Black tossed his head and gave a fierce snort. The time had come to move on, even if he remained unsure which way to go. Somehow, he would find his way out of this place.

He started down a path, knowing he could circle

around the herd of man-beasts. As he moved along, a fresh wind brought with it a familiar smell that stopped him in his tracks. It was the boy. There was fear there, he scented, as well as the smell of fresh blood. The stallion turned his head into the wind and let the telltale signs lead him to where his heart told him he must go—to the boy.

Soon the stallion was close enough to see the fires burning and the gathering of horses and men. His flight instinct warned him to avoid these men who were ruled by creatures that looked like horses but acted like hungry wolves. Still the stallion continued along the path, following the scent in the breeze.

The Black moved down the path, unafraid. He was a stallion, desert-born. What he could not outrun he would fight, and he could stand his own with any. If his enemy could stalk him, he could stalk them, these predators who lived for blood. And if he had to, he would match them in their violence. He had killed horses. He had killed men. If necessary, he would kill again. Let *them* fear *him*.

The sounds of the pounding drums filled the air as he descended the trail. The scent of the burning fire became stronger in his nostrils, but so did the scent of his boy.

Preoccupied with each other, those gathered by the pit did not see the stallion as he crept closer, hiding in the shadows of the trees and rocks. He was a predator now, like his enemy, waiting and watching for the time to move.

The mare was here, too, the Black knew. He could smell her close by. He wondered if she could sense him as well. Then, among the crowd, he could see the boy struggling with a pack of man-beasts.

The stallion did not hesitate. With two quick steps, he bounded into a gallop, trampling the ground and rushing ahead, bearing down on the man-beasts. A cry went up from those in his way as the stallion burst in upon the throng. The boy was there on the ground, alone, just as the stallion had been alone, cornered as he had been cornered. But now they were together, and together they would fight. And together they would win. And together they would escape.

Alec scrambled to his feet among the shouts of men, cries of anger and pain. Then there was a shrill whistle, a drumming of hooves, and like an avenging angel, the Black crashed in upon their enemies. The stallion reared up, higher and higher still, until his raven mane unfurled like a flag in the moonlight, his hooves beating the air, his eyes like lanterns of hate.

Does he even recognize me? Alec thought. "Black," he called. "It's me!" If the stallion heard him, he made no sign of it. Alec was knocked back to the ground as the Black careened past him and burst upon the others, charging back and forth and flailing his hooves.

To get clear, Alec crawled backward until he felt someone taking his arm and lifting him to his feet. It seemed like a gentle gesture, and for an instant Alec thought perhaps help had arrived at last. He turned his head to look over his shoulder, and his hopes collapsed.

It was Medio behind him. The mask had fallen from the mad governor's face, and his sharp eyes glared at Alec. He tried to pull free, but the baby-faced giant easily managed to keep Alec's arms pinned to his sides. He whispered some words Alec did not understand, his tone soft and menacing, his breath foul on Alec's neck.

Alec threw back his head with a grunt but wasn't close enough to connect. Crushed in the man's embrace, Alec felt his feet lift inches off the ground. As Medio carried him to the gate, Alec threw his weight from side to side and kicked his legs. Nothing seemed to help. He was trapped as surely as a fly in a spiderweb.

Just as they reached the entrance to the gate, there was an explosion of hooves. It was the Black. Behind him, two guards lay unconscious on the ground; the rest had scattered. Medio called to the stallion and pushed Alec forward, holding him as a shield between him and the black demon. Alec looked into the Black's eyes, trying to read what he could but seeing only black rage.

Medio shouted fearlessly as the enraged stallion moved upon them, pushing them both back against a pillar and then through the gate, closer to the precipice.

The Black coiled back on his haunches and charged again. Medio spun around. He raised an arm, trying to avoid the blows from the stallion's hooves, and Alec pulled himself free. Medio snarled as Alec escaped but did not try to pursue him. All the man's attention was focused on the Black.

The stallion struck on one side of his cornered prey and then the other, pushing him closer to the edge of the cliff. Medio moved backward, waving his arms and cowering from the blows. In desperation, he tried to break to the side. Tangling his feet, he lost his balance as he came too close to the edge. He seemed to hang in midair for an instant, a look of surprise on his face. Then, with a cry of disbelief, the Lord of Acracia tumbled over the precipice and down into the pit.

A gasp fell over the party of revelers lining the rim of the crater, followed by a great silence. Alec looked out at the masked faces as they stared into the pit. No one moved or made an effort to help their fallen leader.

At the bottom of the slide, Medio clutched his

thigh. He struggled to his feet and limped toward a
doorway in the wall of the arena. Alec watched as one
of the white mares approached Medio. The Acracian
emperor said something and held up his hand. The
mare hesitated a moment, then moved closer.

Medio called out again and reached out to the
mare as if to caress her. She brushed past his hand and
lowered her head to sniff at the fresh blood staining
his bare legs. Then she licked it. Medio suddenly drew
back. He tried to push the mare away but she per-
sisted, licking at the blood and quickly taking hold
with her teeth. Medio struck at her head as she raked
his arm with her teeth. The rest of the herd circled
closer and then moved in to join their sister.

Medio staggered backward until the gray stallion
lunged at him, knocking him to the ground. The fallen
governor stared up in terror as the circle of death tightened in upon him. He cried out and reached for his
sword, but it was already too late.

Alec turned from the awful sight and rushed back
through the gate. The Black stood alone, waiting for
him. The stallion watched Alec approach, then reared
and pawed the air.

Alec stopped short and stood still until the stallion's hooves were on the ground again; then he
stepped in close. The Black snorted but did not move

away as Alec stepped closer and raised his hand to the black mane. He spoke some low words and then, drawing on every ounce of energy he could muster, hurled himself onto the stallion's back. A second later they were off and running. Alec buried his head in his horse's mane, wanting nothing more than to get away, to get anywhere, as long as it was far from here.

16

Escape

The Black carried him at a gallop through the village at the mountaintop, slowing to a trot as they reached the road down the mountain. Again Alec could see the fallen trees, collapsed walls and other signs of the earthquake that had shaken the mountain earlier that evening.

Alec stroked the Black's neck, trying to calm both of their nerves. He could hardly believe what had just happened. Could he have come any nearer to death than he had been only a few minutes ago? If it wasn't for the Black, he would probably be dead right now.

Soon the eastern mountain peaks started to lighten, and Alec realized it must be close to dawn. All his senses told him to escape this place as soon as he could, but he knew they couldn't leave Xeena here, especially after what he'd just seen up at the temple.

Alec took a deep breath and tried to take stock of what he needed to do now. Medio was dead. There was no way to tell whether Spiro and the others would blame the Black for causing his death or spoiling their ceremony. No one had tried to prevent Alec and the Black from escaping the place or made any attempt to pursue them when they left. The entire gathering, even the Acracian guard, had just stood there stunned, as if in a collective trance, while Alec had mounted his horse and ridden off. Surely they'd come out of their stupor before long, and Alec didn't want to be around when they did.

He leaned forward and spoke softly to his horse. They pulled to a stop, and both looked back toward the mountaintop. Alec could see the flaming horse effigy still burning on the distant mountainside. He watched for signs of movement on the road behind him and saw none. Nor could he hear anything but the unnatural silence that always seemed to permeate these woods.

The Black held his head high, his ears pricked. Alec watched the stallion for any signs that the horse sensed something in the wind. After a moment, the stallion dropped his head, seemingly unconcerned. Perhaps Medio's followers weren't as loyal as they were professed to be. Certainly no one seemed to be chasing after him, Alec thought, at least not yet.

Questions raced through his mind, and he forced himself to think ahead. He still had no idea how to get out of this place. Would the guards try to stop them when they passed through the acropolis? Were the citizens of Acracia evacuating the city after the quake, or was the main gate still closed?

They reached the fork in the road, and Alec turned the Black toward Tarta. He could only hope Xeena was still there.

In the distance he could see the tower, and soon they reached the outskirts of the town. Alec found his way to the cottage where Nicholas lived and was relieved to see Xeena in the yard with her grandfather. Nicholas was trying to get the front door back on its hinges. He stopped working when he saw the Black and Alec.

Alec jumped down from his horse's back.

"You found him," Xeena said. "Where was he?"

"Don't ask," he said, "I can't even begin to tell you."

"Come have a glass of water," Nicholas said, leading Alec through the open doorway. "It will clear your thoughts."

Xeena stayed with the Black, who lowered his head and began grazing hungrily on Nicholas's overgrown lawn.

"You were at the temple ceremony?" Nicholas said as they stepped through the open doorway. Alec didn't answer, but the man must have read Alec's expression and guessed the truth. "Then you know," he said.

Inside, the house was in shambles, with piles of broken dishes and glass, collapsed shelves and cracked walls. Alec took a drink of water and felt new strength spiral through his head and body. It made him talkative suddenly, and Nicholas listened as Alec told him what had happened at the temple atop Mt. Atnos.

Nicholas smiled. "So Medio is no more," he said. "The king is dead. Long live the king." He gave Alec a deferential bow of his head. "You will be a wonderful governor, and all Acracia looks forward to your reign."

Alec laughed at the thought.

Nicholas's expression became serious. "That is not a debate, Alec, or a request," he said. "You and the Black were chosen. You cannot insult the gods by refusing to take your place among them now."

"We can't, huh?" Alec said, and laughed again at the absurdity of it all. "Why can't Spiro be chosen? He is the chamberlain."

"True," Nicholas said. "He was the next in line, until your arrival here. But such is Fate. Spiro could never command if you fled the realm. There would be chaos. For Spiro to rule, you would need to meet your fate as Medio did, via the red road—an offering to the sacred mares."

"Chaos?" Alec said. "That would be an improvement from what I've seen around here. This mixed-up paradise of yours could use some chaos."

"Please consider your position," Nicholas said. "You cannot defy the will of the gods."

"Do you seriously think I want to give up my life and stay here, as governor, or king, or guest, or anything else?" Alec said. "And what about Xeena? Do you really believe this is the best place for her?"

Nicholas did not answer, but the mention of Xeena plainly troubled him and he looked vulnerable suddenly. Alec walked back outside and Nicholas followed.

"We have to go," Alec told Xeena. "We have to get out of here."

Xeena looked at him. Her voice was stiff. "We can't leave yet. People could be hurt. They need our help. And what about Popi?"

Alec shook his head. "You don't understand. We have to get out of here. Right now."

Nicholas glanced at Alec, a steely serenity in his expression now, as if he had resolved his inner conflicts and made up his mind. Then he put his hands on Xeena's shoulders and looked her straight in the face. "Alec is right," he said. "You must leave, child."

"I'm no child," Xeena said. "I'm—"

Nicholas gave Xeena a hug. "You are unafraid,

Xeena," he said, "and I respect that. But listen, you must go. It is too late for me. You have drunk only lightly of the water here; perhaps it is not too late for you."

"We have to go now," Alec repeated firmly.

Xeena untangled herself from Nicholas's arms. "I am not going without you," she said stubbornly.

Alec looked at the young man who he now accepted was indeed Xeena's grandfather in the body of a man less than half his age. How that happened, he hadn't a clue, but he had to accept it.

Nicholas shook his head. "I could not join you, even if I wanted to. The effects of Acracian waters come at a price. Without it, not only would the benefits of the blessed nectar be reversed, but also whatever illness, injury or age had been masked by the effects of the water would return, and be compounded." The young-old man sighed wearily. "I suppose no one really knows. No one has ever left Acracia and returned to say otherwise."

"That doesn't matter," Alec said. "We have to try. We are not staying here."

"I don't understand, Popi," Xeena said. "Your family loves you. You have to come with us. You have to try."

"Do not grieve for me, Xeena. I am comfortable here. When my time comes, I will go the way of the others before me."

"But why?" Xeena pleaded.

"I am a citizen of the Acracian realm, loyal in heart, mind, body and soul. Here we do not die from old age or disease, but for loyalty. It is our responsibility to keep in step. If we have violated Nature's law, we must wait for her judgment."

Alec listened to Nicholas. He didn't understand the reasoning, and it didn't matter anyway. There was no more time to waste.

"We have to go, Xeena," he said. "Come on."

The Black suddenly stamped his hooves, lifted his head and shrilled. "Ho," Alec cried.

Approaching the yard was Spiro flanked by the three white mares and the gray stallion from the temple pit. The horses' eyes were alight with hunger, their muzzles smeared with blood.

"Salutations, Governor Alexander," the chamberlain called out. "Your chargers await you."

Nicholas took Xeena by the hand, and they stepped closer to Alec and the Black for protection. Then, at a vocal cue from Spiro, the four horses spread out and took up positions around the black stallion and the three humans huddled in his shadow. The horses moved at a slow, unhurried walk, their noses close to the ground, like slinking wolves, predators zeroing in for the kill.

These were not horses as Alec knew them, and he

couldn't help but be fascinated by the sight. How could he fight creatures he could not understand, horses with human blood on their lips?

The circle tightened. With a savage cry, the Black bolted for Nicholas's cottage, as if trying to draw the flesh-eating horses away from Alec, Xeena and Nicholas. But the mares remained where they were, and only the gray followed. The Black ducked through the open front door of the cottage, and the gray rushed in after him. The sounds of smashing plates and splintering furniture mixed with the screams of the two stallions. A few seconds later, they came bursting outside and the battle spilled into the front yard.

The three mares watched as the Black broke off the fight and circled around one side of the ruined cottage. The gray stallion responded by climbing a ramp made of sections of fallen roof and slinking over to the edge. As the Black came into range beneath him, the gray leaped down upon him like a mountain lion pouncing on its prey. Then both horses were on the ground, rolling and thrashing their hooves as they tried to get up again.

"Popi!" Xeena cried out.

Alec whirled to see Xeena caught between Nicholas and Spiro. Nicholas had her by one arm and Spiro by the other. Both were pulling her in different directions. Alec rushed at Spiro and knocked him to the ground. Nicholas fell upon Spiro and they began to struggle. Instantly the pack of mares returned to claim their captives.

Xeena dashed away as Nicholas and Spiro wrestled each other on the ground. Alec sprang to his feet. There among the horse pack, he saw the shoe-thieving mare from last night. Her attention was focused on Nicholas and Spiro, her lips pulled back in a wolfish snarl. Both Nicholas and Spiro seemed unaware of the mare as she closed on them and moved in for the kill. The two men were fighting on their knees now, each trying to pin the other to the ground.

Without thinking, Alec took a quick step back and leaped astride the mare's back. She immediately reared and Alec leaned forward, his legs wrapped around her neck. He locked his ankles and began squeezing with all his strength.

The mare pounded her forehooves in the dirt and then suddenly stopped her bucking and thrashing. She reeled around, shrilling defiantly. A piercing cry answered her. It was the Black, returning from his combat with the gray, who was now nowhere to be seen.

All three mares turned their attention to the stallion charging into their midst. Spiro and Nicholas continued their fighting, Nicholas pleading desperately for Xeena to stay away. Shoe Thief bucked, then shot into the air.

The Black reared back, plainly startled by seeing Alec astride the mare. Shoe Thief lunged at the Black, and the best Alec could do was swing his free hand at her head to try pushing it away from the Black. She pushed back and fought to take hold of the stallion's neck with her teeth. Alec struck again, and this time the blood-maddened mare turned away from the Black. With one great heaving of her body, she threw herself into the air again. Alec lost his seat and flopped to the ground. In an instant, Xeena was standing over him, giving him a hand and pulling him to his feet.

"Get up," she cried. "It's Popi . . . He pulled me free and then . . ."

Alec looked to where Nicholas and Spiro had been fighting. Both had fallen beneath the mares' hooves. The two mares squealed and sparred with each other as they fought over the broken bodies and bloody, ripped-up clothes.

Alec put his arm around Xeena and turned her away. Only a dozen yards off, the Black was still battling Shoe Thief. She reared up, her lips pulling back to show long, sharp teeth. The Black rose on his hind legs to meet her.

Shoe Thief flicked her head and came at the Black's neck, not trying to take hold this time but nipping almost playfully, letting the stallion feel her teeth, as if it was all just a game. The Black pounded the earth with his hooves. The mare collected herself and stood ready to attack.

There was the sound of onrushing hooves, and Alec spun around to see yet another horse crashing toward them. It was Celera, the albino mare, her head and tail held high. With a defiant war cry, she thundered to a stop, then stepped between the Black and Shoe Thief, her neck arched in disdain. The two other mares trotted over to join their sister and face the albino. Alec took Xeena by the hand and pulled her closer to the Black.

Celera screamed at the mares, and they replied in a chorus of frenzied whinnies and animal snarls as she stood between them and their prey. Celera stood her ground, keeping the other mares back, as if to protect Alec, Xeena and the Black from the flesh-eating white sisters.

The mares hesitated before challenging the ruby-eyed albino. One finally lowered her head and thrust forward. Celera easily sidestepped the charge and let fly with her hind hooves. The white mare crashed to the ground with a squeal of pain. After another moment's hesitation, her sisters tried to move closer. Celera stamped the ground threateningly and then lunged, striking out with the skill of a practiced warrior.

As the mares fought among themselves, Alec pulled the Black away and swung onto his back. He grabbed Xeena by the arm and pulled her up behind him. "Hang on," he cried over his shoulder.

The stallion whirled and took off, racing for the road as fast as a horse carrying two riders could run.

"Go, Black, go!" Alec cried.

They startled a herd of goats as they zoomed past. As they turned down the road to the acropolis, Alec heard something behind him, the defiant call of a horse. He turned to see Celera racing after them. Alec urged the Black faster, hoping beyond hope that Xeena could manage to hang on as the stallion lengthened his stride on the open road. He glanced back over his shoulder again. The albino was still there, chasing after them and getting closer. At least there was no sign of the other mares on the road behind her. That was something to be grateful for.

As they reached the outskirts of the acropolis, Alec could see more signs of destruction from the earth tremor here—broken columns, collapsed pillars and stone debris. The Black had to slow down, but so would Celera. What the Black couldn't get around, he jumped over. Somehow both Alec and Xeena remained on his back.

Celera closed in behind them as they reached an open field that led to the acropolis. Alec spotted a fissure that had been rent in the wall from top to bottom. It was a miracle. The earthquake had opened a passageway to the outside!

This was their only chance, and Alec turned the Black toward it. The stallion saw it, too, and needed no further urging from Alec. He knew where he was going now. The albino kept up her pursuit. Unburdened by one rider, much less two, Celera was soon only a length away and closing.

Celera cried out as she narrowed the gap between them. It was not a war cry this time but a haunting, forlorn, almost pleading sound. Whatever it meant to the Black, he did not stop.

Soon the two horses were running neck and neck toward the jagged opening in the wall. Careening through the passage, they emerged on the stretch of grass lying between the wall and the moatlike canal bordering the city. At last the Acracian walls were behind them, and they were free. What a relief!

The two horses rushed to a place where the canal narrowed to little more than a stream. Reaching the edge at the same instant, the runners leaped into the air, flying across the enchanted waters to the other side.

Out of the corner of his eye, Alec could see something happen to Celera as they touched down on the opposite bank. A whooshing sound filled his ears, like something bursting into flames, much like the sound Alec had heard when the wooden horse caught fire.

The mare didn't fall, but something was clearly wrong with her. She stumbled to a stop. The Black, too, stumbled and slowed to a halt, breathing hard. Alec let go and both he and Xeena tumbled to the ground, rolling through the grass.

All at once, Alec's left ankle throbbed with pain, the one he thought he had twisted days before. As Nicholas had warned, all the pain that Alec hadn't felt for the past few days was returning with a vengeance. His entire body ached as if he had suddenly been struck by an intense case of altitude sickness.

Alec looked up at the Black standing unsteadily beside him, clearly shaken, his body trembling. Xeena lay groaning on the ground. The stallion threw back his head and whinnied to Celera as she tried to come closer.

The mare teetered on her legs and could barely move. She was still standing but was also transforming before Alec's very eyes, aging years in seconds and then even faster. It was as if she were drying up, as if all the moisture was draining from her body. Suddenly her magnificent white coat seemed to turn to paper, wrinkling and cracking and finally dissolving into a heap of dust.

"Alec," Xeena called. "Are you okay?"

Alec heard Xeena but he didn't turn to see the girl. His eyes remained fixed, as the Black's were, on the pile of dust that was all that remained of the albino mare.

"Did you see . . ." Alec started to say. He blinked, still disbelieving his own eyes. It was true, he realized. Celera was gone.

"What happened to the albino?" Xeena said. "Did she fall in the water?"

Alec shook his head. "She just . . . vanished." He pointed to all that was left of the mare, little more than ashes and dust. The Black paced back and forth, waiting and watching, as if trying to reason what was happening. The stallion cautiously approached the ashen remains of Celera, sniffed the ground, then whinnied and pulled back.

A mountain breeze blew up around them suddenly. The breath of wind picked up the pile of dust, and the particles flew into the air, becoming a grayish puff. Alec watched as the dust swirled along like a tiny dust devil, floating back across the stream to the other side. Once there, the swirl turned inside itself, becoming what looked like a cluster of windblown paper, quickly taking on thickness and shape and the form of a white horse. Once returned to the other side of the river, the dust reassembled into Celera, just as quickly as she had dissolved.

The reconstituted albino mare reared up and

shrilled to the Black. The stallion cried an answer and charged to the river's edge but did not jump. He threw back his head and called to the mare again.

Celera stood still, watching him silently. Then, with one last, plaintive cry, she spun around and ran off to vanish beyond the city walls.

The Black watched her go. He cried again, but no answer came. The stallion paced back and forth on the embankment, neighing wildly and pawing the ground as if anxious to jump across the river to the other side.

Alec tried to call out to his horse, but he could barely find the breath to speak. In a minute, the Black stopped his pacing, raised his head and sniffed the wind. Then he turned to where Alec lay sprawled on the ground.

"Black," Alec managed to call, his voice a hoarse croak. He tried to stand up, but his legs felt incredibly weak and collapsed beneath him. Crawling over to an outcropping of rocks, he pulled himself high enough so he could mount the Black again. Once he was on the stallion's back, he gave Xeena a hand and swung her up behind him.

Alec felt weak, spent. His body ached and his sore ankle throbbed. He looked around him, wondering what direction was home, finally letting the Black decide which way they should go.

17

Home

How long they wandered in the woods Alec wasn't sure. He felt dazed, but the pain in his leg kept him awake. He and Xeena barely spoke as they rode along, hunched together over the stallion's back. From time to time, Alec could hear her weeping behind him, and once he heard Xeena calling her grandfather's name softly to herself. Alec didn't know what to say, so he didn't say anything. The Black was strong enough for all of them, carrying his riders up one trail and down another, sometimes stopping in his tracks to retrace his steps and take a different turn.

Finally they emerged from a tree tunnel to a gently sloping field. At the bottom of the field was what looked like a road. Alec lifted his head to the sky, and from the position of the sun, he could see that it was already early afternoon.

"Whoa," he called to the Black as the stallion started to break into a quicker pace in the open field.

"I think it's a road," Xeena said, her voice excited suddenly.

Alec pulled the Black to a stop. Xeena hopped off and Alec slid gently to the ground, his legs still shaky beneath him.

"We didn't pass by this field before," Alec said, "but I bet that road leads somewhere if we just keep following it down the mountain." He took a step and staggered as his injured leg buckled beneath him.

"You better ride," Xeena said. "I'll walk."

Alec got set to remount, but before he did, he glanced over his shoulder to where they'd just been. The mouth of the tree tunnel seemed to have vanished, swallowed up by the forest as if it had never existed.

Alec pulled himself onto the Black's back, and they started down the mountain. He still felt dazed and thankfully was able to keep the stallion to a slow pace. Xeena walked beside them in silence and apparently deep in thought.

It was Cleo that found them, Xeena's sleepy-eyed pony. Amazingly, she was still tacked up in saddle and bridle, exactly as she had been when they left her at the falls three days ago. She was sauntering up the path in the other direction, jogging lightly toward them as if she'd just come outside for an afternoon stroll. The mare whinnied as she saw them. Xeena dashed ahead to greet her horse and threw her arms around the mare's neck.

"I can't believe this," Alec said as he joined her. "What is Cleo doing here? Didn't she go back home after we went into the falls? Has she been out here all the time we were gone?"

"I guess so," Xeena answered, glad to be with her horse again. She leaned her forehead against the mare's neck to breathe in the smell of her. Alec watched her and smiled. At least they were closer to home now than they had been an hour ago.

Xeena swung herself into the saddle, and a minute later they all were making good time down the trail. The path ahead wound past rocks and trees, at one point edging along a steep mountain pass Alec had never seen before. At last the path straightened and widened to a dirt road. Soon Alec could see the monastery walls in the distance and the film crew's trucks parked in a row outside the visitors' compound. There was movement around them, people from the crew.

At last it was over, Alec thought. The long and terrible journey through the lost city had come to an end. He felt exhausted, too tired to think of food or anything else but lying down and going to sleep.

Soon they were passing through the gate to the

compound. No one seemed to pay them much attention. The gaffers and electricians who had been hanging out around their trucks barely gave them any notice at all. It wasn't that Alec cared or expected a big reception, but hadn't the crew been alerted about Xeena and Alec going missing? Hadn't their unexplained absence caused some concern among the crew?

Reaching the Black's tent, Alec carefully dismounted and put the Black in his stall. Then he set to fixing the stallion's feed and water. The Black waited and watched him patiently as Alec hobbled around the tent. There was a look of dark sadness in the stallion's eyes, and Alec spoke to his horse in singsong to brighten their spirits. He gave the Black a few swipes with a soft brush, then stepped out of the stall and sat down on a tack trunk to catch his breath.

Xeena had walked Cleo to her own tent, and a few minutes later she returned. Karst was with her. The sight of Xeena's dad startled Alec. For a moment, Alec thought he was back in Tarta looking at Nicholas. Then Karst put on a playful smile, and when the man spoke, Alec knew that this was the real Karst and no one else.

"How was your walk?" Karst said in his thick Greek accent. "I hear you take a fall."

"How was our walk?" Alec said, hardly believing his ears. Alec glanced at Xeena, but her expression revealed nothing. "Didn't she tell you what happened to us?"

Karst looked at Alec's ankle. "Not broken?"

"I don't think so," Alec said. "Maybe I sprained it."

"We get you fixed up with nurse. Be good as new, no time."

"Yes, but . . . Karst, didn't you get the message about what happened to us? Haven't you been wondering where we've been? Wasn't any sort of search made?"

Karst looked perplexed. "Why search? You not gone so long. Maybe two, three hours. You okay?" Karst said, a hint of concern coming into his voice.

Alec looked at his friend, the shock he was feeling surely visible on his face. "Two or three hours?" Alec said. "Are you saying this is still Tuesday?"

"You okay?" Karst repeated. "You hit your head? Yes, Tuesday. Crew on break; we sit tight, still waiting for director. Chopper broke down. He be here tomorrow." Karst pointed at Alec's swollen ankle. "You take it easy. We get you to nurse's station and then you rest."

Xeena glanced at Alec, and she shook her head slightly, as if signaling him to stop. "Go ahead," she said. "I'll stay with the Black."

Karst unclipped his walkie-talkie from his belt and put in a call to Jeff. The young Australian soon drove up in his golf cart. "Heard you had a little accident," Jeff said. "Hop in and I'll take you to Lana. She can get you fixed up."

Alec climbed into the golf cart beside Jeff, and they drove to the nurse's tent.

The nurse washed and bandaged Alec's ankle, then sent him on his way with a walking cane and a pocket full of extra-strength aspirin. "That'll do until we can get you back down the mountain tomorrow night," she said.

Jeff was waiting outside in his golf cart as Alec left the tent. "Where to now, boss?" Jeff said amiably. "Do you want to go back to your room?"

"Think I better check on my horse," Alec said.

Jeff nodded and eased the golf cart in that direction. "Well, you missed a good card game after lunch," Jeff said as the cart hummed along. "We are having another one tonight, if you're up for it."

Alec glanced at Jeff a moment and then turned away. He still felt dazed by all that had happened, and he knew it probably still showed on his face.

"You feeling all right?" Jeff said. "You look sort of sick."

"I'm okay," Alec said. "It's just . . . this has been the strangest day. I don't think I'll ever be the same again."

Jeff laughed. "Oh, you will be all right," he

said. "I didn't hear how you took your fall. What happened?"

"I'm not sure," Alec said. There was something in him that wanted very much to confide in another person about what he had seen, if only to try to assemble some kind of sense out of it. Besides that, he didn't have the energy to think up an alternative alibi.

Alec started talking and Jeff listened easily. They arrived at the tent. Jeff switched off the motor, a half smile on his face, plainly not sure if he was being kidded or not. Even to Alec's ears, the story he told sounded incredible. Perhaps that was because they were here, safe in the monastery compound surrounded by tents, trucks and their fellow crew, not lost in the wandering woods around Mt. Atnos. Alec recounted what he could, though he intentionally left some parts out, mainly the part about Nicholas's recovered youth and the horror he had seen at the temple of Diomedes.

They sat there in the cart for many moments until Alec finished his story. Then Jeff asked him straight out, "You wouldn't be pulling my leg, would you, Alec? Is this some kind of joke?"

Alec shook his head. "I wish it was. The woods here are . . ."

"What? Magical? Like a magic forest? I don't know, Alec. This sounds like something right out of

Alice in Wonderland. Maybe one of the monks slipped some forest mushroom into your eggs this morning. It is a great yarn, though."

Alec looked at Jeff. What was the use? he thought. Who could believe such a far-fetched tale? And Alec had not one shred of evidence to back up his story. He thanked Jeff for the ride. "No worries, mate," Jeff said lightly as he glided off in his cart.

Alec stepped into the Black's tent. Xeena was idly cleaning some tack that didn't need it, just to keep busy. Alec told her about Jeff's reaction to the story of what happened on their walk that afternoon. "He thought I was making it all up," Alec said. "I don't know what else I expected."

Xeena shook her head. "I know what my dad would say if I told him."

Alec nodded. "Hard to believe we'll both be out of here tomorrow and all this will just be a memory. I just wish I understood. . . ."

Xeena's walkie-talkie crackled to life, and Karst's voice broke in over their conversation. Xeena stood up. "I better go," she said stoically, the serious kid back on the job.

"Take it easy, girl," Alec said.

"You too."

Alec looked in on the Black, then sat on his tack trunk and tried to read a little. He began to feel tired again, so he set up his stable cot to lie down for a minute and take a quick nap. In minutes he was fast asleep, and he stayed that way for the rest of the afternoon, through dinner and long into the night.

Everyone was up extra early the next morning. Bateman had choppered in at first light, and shooting was supposed to be completed by noon, at least according to the schedule Alec had seen. He, the Black and most of the crew would be leaving the monastery shortly thereafter.

Alec's head hurt a little for some reason, but at least his ankle wasn't bothering him too much. He fed and watered the Black, then led him outside so he could stretch his legs.

Jeff caught up to Alec as they circled the animal tents. "Feeling better this morning?" he asked. "How's the head?"

"Yeah, I'm okay. Thanks. But don't we have to rehearse or something for the scene we're supposed to do? I'm still not sure. . . ."

Jeff smiled. "No worries, mate," he said. "Your scene should be a snap. We'll block it out when we get to the location. For now, just go get into costume. We'll be ready for you when you're ready."

An hour later, Alec and the Black were suited up in their Alexander and Bucephalus outfits and waiting with Karst and the rest of the crew on the set. It was the same location they had used before, the place with the spectacular mountain backdrop only a few minutes from the compound.

The place looked like a construction site. Black cables snaked across the ground between humming generators and the sound and lighting equipment. The crew called back and forth, adjusting camera tripods and positioning stands of lights. Two separate camera teams had taken up vantage points along the route. Bateman shuttled back and forth between cameras in his golf cart, crouching down and peering through the lenses, backing up and moving from side to side, checking every possible angle.

Jeff waved to Alec and jogged over. "We are about ready," he said. "This is the layout. Do you see Xeena over there?" He pointed to a spot a couple hundred yards away where Xeena and Cleo were positioned up the hill. "Think of her as a marker. Stiv wants you to lope along straight toward her. The first camera team will track you from the start. When you pass the second team, you should turn to them and point as if you have just noticed some riders in the distance. Got it?"

"Sounds simple enough."

"Places, everyone," called the assistant director over a bullhorn. "Quiet on the set."

Another assistant stepped in front of the camera

holding a black slate clapboard. "*Young Alexander,* scene twenty-one, take one."

"Action!"

Alec urged the Black ahead, and they loped toward Xeena and Cleo, turning and pointing as they passed the second camera team.

"Cut, cut, cut," Bateman called over from a bull-horn behind him. "Back it up. Do it again."

Alec turned the Black around, and they returned to the start marker where Karst was waiting for them.

"Okay," Bateman called out after a moment. "Let's take it from the top. A little faster this time." The assistant with the clapboard stepped in front of the camera again. "*Young Alexander,* scene twenty-one, take two."

"Action!" Alec and the Black took off again, Alec pushing the stallion into a slow gallop. "Cut! Do it again," came the orders over the bullhorn.

Alec thought he and the Black were doing everything that was asked of them, but Bateman wanted more footage, so they kept retaking the scene. Every few takes, the camera crews tried a new shooting angle. As much time was spent adjusting cameras and lights between takes as the actual filming. Finally, after fifteen takes, the director seemed satisfied. "That's a keeper, people," Bateman said. "Set up for the next shot."

Alec and the Black started back to the wardrobe tent to get out of their costumes. They were through for the day, and now all they had to do was get packed up and ready for the trip down the mountain. It felt good to be busy and working, Alec thought, good to not think too much about what he had seen, or thought he'd seen, in the Acracian woods yesterday.

All at once, he heard someone calling his name from behind. It was none other than the director, Stiv Bateman. Alec pulled the Black to a stop and swung down from the saddle.

Bateman glanced at the Black and then turned to Alec. "Can I walk with you a minute?"

"Sure," Alec said. "It'd be a pleasure."

"I wanted to thank you for your help on the shoot," Bateman said. "The footage looks great, and I think the Black has a future in pictures if he wants it. But there is something else I'd like to talk to you about. Jeff told me an interesting story this morning, a story he says you told him yesterday, something about a lost city in the forest. Were they ruins?"

Me and my big mouth, Alec thought. But the cat was already out of the bag, and there was no sense in being coy about it now. He spoke up and tried to be as honest as he could. "They weren't ruins," Alec said. "It was a city, like an ancient Greek city, a place unlike anything I've ever seen."

"Tell me about it," Bateman said. His expression was intent, his eyes focused. Alec repeated the version of the story he had told Jeff. Bateman walked beside him and listened quietly all the way back to the Black's tent.

"I don't expect you to believe me," Alec said at last, "but since you asked . . ."

"Believe you? Who says I don't believe you?"

The director's reaction was not at all what Alec had expected. He was actually taking Alec seriously. "I just figured . . ."

Bateman laughed jovially. "Why not? Life is still a mystery to me. And you don't look like the sort of guy who would make up a yarn like that just for fun. I think I'd like to see this lost, time-wandering city of yours for myself."

"Seriously?"

"Sure. It sounds fascinating. Don't know how I'd get in there, though. It was hard enough getting permission to film here at the monastery. I might try it guerilla-style, like we used to do back in film school. Go in light, take some money for bribes. It just might work." Bateman looked at his watch. "Gotta go, kid," he said. "And thanks for sharing. If I go, I'll let you know how it turns out."

Alec led the Black to the tent entrance and then turned and watched the director hustling off back to the set, already barking orders into his walkie-talkie. He wondered if Bateman was really serious about what he had said. Bateman did have a reputation for shooting in the most out-of-the-way places imaginable, in deep jungle and at the bottom of the sea, so it made sense that he might be tempted to do what he said he wanted to do.

For the next hour or two, Alec busied himself packing and getting the Black ready for the van ride down the mountain. Xeena gave him a hand stowing his gear in the van, and he told her about his talk with Bateman.

"I guess some people are like that," she said. "I wouldn't go back into those woods for a million dollars. But to tell you the truth, right now I am starting to think it might have been just some incredible dream after all."

"If it was a dream," Alec said, "we were in it together."

Xeena nodded. "That makes me feel better for some reason. Let's leave it at that."

"Fine with me," he said. Alec stepped over to the tack trunk. "Can you give me a hand with this? My ankle still hurts a little."

Xeena smiled. "Sure," she said, taking up the other end of the trunk.

"Thanks," Alec said. "At least I know I didn't imagine this twisted ankle of mine."

An hour later, the Black was safely loaded up and Alec was sitting in the van's passenger seat as Karst eased the van out the driveway and through the monastery gate. Xeena was riding with Cleo and some of the other horses in Thomas's van, so it was just the two of them. Karst waved to the monks standing watch, but the sullen-eyed men took no notice of him. He shook his head and laughed. "Friendly guys."

Alec leaned forward in his seat and turned to look out his window to the peaks of Mt. Atnos, now shrouded in thick clouds. He wondered again about Celera and the white mares. Were they still there, grazing on the lush grass in their sacred pastures? He thought about Cyrene and the temple of Diomedes and wondered if the citizens of Acracia were rebuilding their city walls. Or had chaos fallen upon the realm, as Nicholas had foretold? A gentle wind drifted through the open window, and Alec heard the sounds of singing birds. For an instant, he thought he could hear the faint, faraway strains of a handheld harp playing a melody from another time. Taking a deep breath, he leaned back in his seat and turned his mind to the road ahead.

◆ ◆ ◆

One cloudy afternoon, several months later, Alec was sitting at his desk in the office of the stallion barn at Hopeful Farm finishing up paying feed bills. It had been some time since he'd even thought about the *Young Alexander* shoot and all that had happened to him and the Black when they were there. With all of his scenes completed, Alec had ended up spending only a few more days in Thrace. The trip home had been painless, first-class all the way, and Alec had quickly settled back into life at Hopeful Farm.

After filling out the last check and addressing the envelope, he stood up from his desk and walked to the window. Outside he could see a pair of foals playing tag in the late autumn sun. Their dams stood nearby in the shade of an oak. He watched them a moment, then took a seat on the office couch. Picking up a newspaper from the coffee table, he scanned the headlines and then turned to the entertainment section to see if there was an interesting movie playing at the local theater. Before he could turn to the listings page, a headline caught his eye:

STIV BATEMAN MISSING IN BULGARIA
Stiv Bateman, renowned screen director of such epic blockbusters as *Underworlds, Amazon Beaming,* and *Beyond Mars,* has been reported missing while location-scouting in a

little-known area of Thracian Bulgaria. The director had recently returned to Thrace after completing postproduction work in Los Angeles on his latest film, *Young Alexander,* a much anticipated work about the early life of Alexander the Great that is due to open next week. Bateman's last communication with the outside world was more than three days ago, and it is feared he is lost and may not be on hand for the opening of his new film. The region where Bateman was last seen is one of the least explored areas of Europe, unmapped and obscured by clouds most of the year. Local district sources say that the eccentric director was traveling in a restricted, unsafe area without permission.

The newspaper fell from Alec's hands and hit the floor. Without thinking, he stood up and walked over to the stallion barn. He picked up a halter and lead shank, then stepped outside again.

"I'm going to check some fences," Alec called to Deb, the barn manager, as he left the tack room. "I'll be right back."

"Okay, boss," Deb said.

The fences didn't need checking, and both he and Deb knew it, but Alec wanted an excuse to get away from the farm for a few minutes. He figured a ride with the Black to a friendly neighbor's back property might give him some time to reflect.

It had been an effort, but so far he had done a pretty good job of putting behind him what had happened to him in the woods around Mt. Atnos and keeping his mind focused on everything he needed to do here at the farm. He hadn't even tried to tell his parents or anyone else about his adventures in the lost city. Now, with the news about Bateman's disappearance, it all came thundering back.

Alec jogged out to the upper pasture where the Black was spending his afternoons these days. Soon he and the stallion were winding their way along a back trail into the woods. As they rode over the soft grass, Alec remembered what he had read about Diomedes since he'd been home. The local library had had hardly any information on him. The only reference to the demigod Diomedes of Thrace was a short paragraph in a kids' book on Greek mythology. It was all there, though, and the words had chilled Alec's blood as he read them: the flesh-eating horses, Diomedes's tyranny and his ultimate death at the hands of his own mares.

The Black carried Alec all the way to a field beyond the woods and a small pond that was a favorite getaway spot for both of them. Alec dismounted and stood beside his horse. The Black slopped his tongue over the back of Alec's sweaty neck.

"What am I, a salt lick?" Alec said, pushing the stallion's head away. "Or are you just working up to the big bite, like one of your girlfriends? Drink some water from the pond if you want something to drink."

They walked to the water's edge. The stallion bent his head to sip from the shallows, swishing his tail in contentment.

Alec thought about Bateman and wondered if he would ever return. Had Stiv really been swept back in time to the lost city among the wandering trees, as he, Xéena and the Black had been? Was the director being made a guest of the realm at that very moment, wondering at the marvels of the acropolis and the lush gardens of Acracia? What would someone like Stiv make of it all? The thought made Alec smile. Bateman would probably love it. At least for a time.

Afterword

Much of the folklore referenced in this story is based on known history, legends and myths. Alexander's Bucephalus was believed by many to be a direct descendant of Diomedes's sacred mares. There were a Sybaris and a Croton in ancient times. The Sybaris cavalry included dancing horses, and they were defeated in battle when the Croton pipers played the horses' favorite dancing music. In Thrace to this day, folktales exist about forests with wandering trees that can hide anything and anyone, and about poisonous rivers and pools of water that will madden any animal or person who drinks from them. Incitatus, the Roman emperor Caligula's horse, was an elected priest and member of the Council of Rome. He ate from an ivory manger, drank from a golden pail and had eighteen attendants. Celer, owned by the Roman emperor Verus, ate nothing but almonds and raisins and was stabled in a suite of apartments in the emperor's palace.

SF

Steven Farley, the third of Walter and Rosemary Farley's four children, was born in Reading, Pennsylvania. He was brought up near there and in Venice, Florida. In both places, there was always a horse in the backyard. *The Young Black Stallion,* cowritten with his father, was Steven's first novel. He followed it up with several more Black Stallion novels, including *The Black Stallion and the Shape-shifter,* which first explored the author's fascination with the great horses of myth.

Steven studied journalism at New York University and has worked as a writer and editor for magazines and TV. Currently he divides his time between New York, Florida, and Mexico.